Other books by the author

My Life at First Try
Short, Vigorous Roots (with Susan O'Neill)
An Accidental American Odyssey
Condensed to Flash: World Classics (with Susan O'Neill)

The Most Excellent Immigrant

A Story Collection

Mark Budman

Livingston Press
University of West Alabama

ISBN 13: 978-1-60489-334-2 trade paper

Library of Congress Control Number: 2022941954

Typesetting and page layout: Cassidy Pedram
Proofreading: Brooke Barger, Joe Taylor
Cover art, design, and layout: McKenna Darley, Cassidy Pedram (Back cover)

Author photo:

These stories appeareed in the following magaines

Stick Figures in Paradise, *The London Magazine, 2019*
Here Comes the Sun. A Divus Story as Here Comes the Sun. A Remastered Divus Story, *Potomac Review, 2020*
Low Flying Children, *Catapult, 2020*
Tick Tack. You are Dead, *Failbetter, 2018*
The Invisible Man, *Witness, 2019*

Contents

Pillow 1.3

The certified interpreter of dreams and afflictions draws a green stick figure with a sad stub of a crayon. "This is you," he explains to his granddaughter. The interpreter draws a smaller stick figure next, with an equally diminutive purple crayon. "That's your *kukla*. *Kukla* is a doll in Russian."

The girl repeats *kukla* obediently. She points with her finger. "Green hair. Purple hair. Very pretty." She claps.

The stick hair is not quite pretty, but the interpreter never refuses a compliment from any quarters. "Do you want me to draw your sister?"

"No, no, no. Only me."

"How old are you?"

"Two."

"How old is your sister?"

"One."

"But aren't you twins?"

"Yep. Twins."

The interpreter is patient. That's a part of both of his jobs descriptions. He draws another green stick figure, identical to the first. They *are* identical twins, so he's not cheating. Then he draws a much bigger figure, in black. The figure is mostly bald but has a luxuriant mustache. "This is *Deda*. Grandfather."

He draws a horizontal line attached to the figure. "That's *Deda*'s gun. To protect you."

The twin's mother, the interpreter's daughter, is nursing the other twin in the bedroom upstairs. The interpreter and his wife are babysitters, maids, cooks, laundry attendants, and chauffeurs at his daughter's household. They spend five days and nights a week here and go home to Boston for the weekends.

The interpreter's daughter comes back into the room, and the interpreter goes upstairs to his office, to his paying job. While his wife spends 100% of her time helping with the grandkids, he spends only 50% of his. He negotiated that much.

His daughter and her husband are generous enough to give him an office in their house to use over the weekdays. A powerful nor'easter paints the outdoors surreal white. The interpreter's happy he need not drive. He's happy the house still has power though the trees keep losing their limbs to the wind and heavy snow, and the wires could be next. It's hard to operate a computer with no juice.

He puts on his headset and smiles into the camera. They trained him how to smile. Sincere and business-like at the same time. His bosses are strict and check on him all the time. Remotely, of course.

"Hi. My ID number is 555-123456. I'm your Russian video interpreter."

He wears a business shirt and sweatpants. Since he's seated at his desk, they only see his top half.

Mark Budman

A few hours after the workday, in bed, he has one of his usual nightmares. He's a doctor talking to a patient in her hospital bed.

"Do you know that they found you unconscious on the floor?"

The patient glares at him. "Of course, they found me unconscious on the floor. That's because I was unconscious on the floor... Wait a minute... I know you. You're not really a doctor. You're an impostor.... I saw you in my nightmares. You're the interpreter of dreams...."

In the morning, after sitting with the kids for a couple of hours, the interpreter goes back to work. Some of his patients are recent immigrants and haven't learned English yet. Some are old-timers who have been in this country for ten, twenty years or more. Almost as long as the interpreter himself. They will never learn English.

The doctor tells him the patients' names and the interpreter greets them in Russian.

Now, an old female patient is clapping in delight. "The man on the TV knows my name!" She's thin as a Popsicle stick. Her eyes are as dull as an old butter knife. Her hair is disheveled. Not pretty.

The interpreter is super patient. That's a part of one of his job descriptions, though the word 'super' is only implied. He doesn't want to get fired. At his age, he won't find another job. He interprets the woman's words dutifully but only in English: "The man on the TV knows my name!"

The doctor doesn't laugh. Though young, she looks tired. She might have little kids at home. *Her* babysitter draws stick figures for them. *Her* babysitter's thoughts are somewhere else. It's only a paying job for *her*.

On Friday, on his way home to Boston, the interpreter stops at a single-story antique store on Route 9 East, identical to every other antique store along the road. His wife is already home now. She took a train.

He's never visited an antique store before. The interpreter has recently paid over two thousand bucks for removing two broken air conditioners and isn't in the mood for spending more. He's never been interested not just in antique stores but in any antiques. Period. What's the point in buying a previously owned thing and paying more than the new one cost?

But this store grabs his attention. The gridlocked traffic is slow, so he notices that there is a bust of Vladimir Lenin displayed on a stand next to the door. He drives in the right lane, so it's easy to stop. The interpreter touches the bust with his middle finger. It doesn't look or feel like marble. Something cheap. Most probably terracotta. He can't find the price sticker, so he goes inside to inquire.

Lenin wasn't as bad as Stalin, who sent his grandparents to Siberia. The Russian historian Roy Medvedev estimated the number of victims of Stalin's regime at 40 million people. In the interpreter's family, Stalin stands one step below Hitler on the hate scale. Lenin sits several steps below, but the interpreter is curious.

Once inside, the interpreter changes his mind about asking the bust price or otherwise bothering the saleswoman. What would he do with the bust? Break it? Spit on it? Threw stones at it? No. Let someone else have it.

In the corner of the room, there is an emperor-sized four-poster bed, piled high with quilts and pillows of all colors of the rainbow. They all look appealing, but one of them, square, pitch-black, with flaming-red needlepoint depicting the Russian Imperial two-headed eagle, speaks to his heart. It looks dreamy as all pillows should, but most don't. He doesn't need it. Neither his daughters nor his wife needs it. As for the twins, their interests are unpredictable at their age.

He won't sleep on it, he decides, but use it as objet

d'art; in the room inaccessible to his granddaughters, of course, or they would take it apart before he blinks.

The pillow is only $49.99 plus tax. A bargain in the world of antiques, as far as he knows. He pays cash.

"Why do we need it?" his wife asks when he shows her the pillow.

A few years ago, when they had come to Boston from the semi-rural area of Upstate New York, they traded their four-bedroom house in the best part of town for the two-bedroom condo less than half as expansive but twice as expensive. They wanted to be closer to their married daughters who were by now old Bostonians.

The condo is situated in a converted turn of the twentieth century mansion, currently subdivided into seven properties, each with a tiny parking spot, a luxury in overcrowded Boston. Their condo takes up a section of two floors at the end of the building, with the neighbors behind the thin wall and above the ceiling. The floors are connected by a black ironwork spiral staircase that took some time to get used to but that looks vaguely castle-like.

The interpreter loves to stop inside the staircase after a few steps up, when he can see nothing but the white walls, and hear nothing but his own breath, and to imagine himself a baron or a count rushing toward the waiting countess on a bed covered by silk sheets, in a floor-length silk dress, a countess whose face is covered by a veil but whose eyes shine through like two LED candles.

Once he talked about the stairs to one of the patients he was interpreting for. They were waiting for the doctor who had told them he would be back in a minute.

About ten minutes into the small talk, the patient, a woman a few years older than the interpreter, said: "You speak Russian like a TV anchor."

The interpreter was compelled to return the favor

somehow. He said the first thing that came to mind. He learned a long time ago that this was the best way to be social. "The spiral staircase makes my house look like a castle in the skies."

The woman laughed. "And I live in section 8, a subsidized apartment. It's like the eighth heaven. Too good to be true, but still nothing like the regular seven heavens."

Back Upstate, the interpreter and his wife used to be surrounded by owner-occupied houses and had lawyers and doctors for neighbors. Now, the neighbors are primarily renters, mostly students. Unlike lawyers and doctors, they still have the strength to party.

"Why do we need it?" his wife asks when he shows her the newly acquired pillow.

"Why do we need anything besides the basics?"

"Don't you philosophize with me." She looks tired. Too many hours, days, and nights without sleep, watching the twins.

"I'm not philosophizing. I'm trying to answer your question. It's not the question of needs but wants."

"Why would you want something that has no value?"

"It does have value. $49.99 plus tax. A bargain in the world of antiques."

She closes her eyes. "OK. It's your money."

"It's our money."

The interpreter takes a pic of the pillow and posts it on Facebook and Twitter. He realizes that bragging about his purchases is childish, but he can't help it. The pic was badly lit and ill-composed, but he got two "likes" on each platform.

He decides that the shooting angle is wrong. Rearranging the pillow, he finds a lump inside. He palpates it carefully. It feels like a box. He takes a pocketknife, cuts the stitches, and pulls out a small wooden jewelry box. It's locked, but he Googles how-to, and picks the lock with two

Mark Budman

paper clips. It's a simple lock anyway.

Inside the box, he discovers seven of the largest pearls he has ever seen. Deep yellowish-orange pearls reflect his open-mouthed face. He takes a ruler and measures them. 13 millimeters each. Probably would cost a fortune if they are natural. But who would hide faux jewelry in a pillow? From the kids? From the spouse? From the IRS?

$49.99 plus tax, huh. A bargain in the world of antiques.

He tells no one about the pearls, not even his wife, not his daughters, not his grandkids.

His wife would probably ask him to find the rightful owner, his daughters would advise to sell them quietly and put the money in the trust, and the toddlers would fight among themselves how to divide the pearls between their dolls. The interpreter puts the jewels back, hides the box inside the pillow again, and sews the pillow back as carefully as he can.

A couple of weeks later, the doorbell rings at his condo. There is an older man and a younger woman on the threshold. The man, stooped and sour-faced, looks hardly taller than his companion.

But the interpreter's eyes are caught by the woman. Her skin is the color of fresh milk with a good measure of blood. A diamond stud pierces her left ear. Her gaze probes the inner layers of the interpreter's brain. She oozes the charisma of a Hollywood starlet, a Twitter-savvy politician, or a real estate saleswoman of the month. Some could call it charisma. Russians call it *simpatichnaya*.

Behind the couple, in the next yard, half-fenced and wooded, a beautiful bluebird is making an indecent proposal to his mate on a limb. A flock of wild turkeys, including a gangly teenager, is watching. As all real Bostonians know all too well, wild turkeys and geese are common in this part of

Boston, to the detriment of traffic, and the detriment of the street cleaners dealing with the bloody remains.

Whether or not the human couple is surprised by the wildlife of a metropolis, the interpreter will never find out.

The woman, who stands in front of the man, flashes a wide smile, showing off her shiny, sharp, exceedingly white teeth, extends her hand, and says *dobry den'*. You don't need to be a certified medical interpreter who works with Russian patients to know that it means "good day" in Russian.

Mark Budman

Penelopa and
Her Odysseus

At the precise moment when spring was turning into summer, Piotr Osipovich Voronin, Russian by birth, American by necessity, was ready to die. About ninety percent ready, give or take, though he wasn't much of a giving person.

He had failed his quest, his Odyssey, and now, holding onto the light pole on Brighton Beach Avenue with both hands, he contemplated his options. Drowning would be too damsel-in-distress, too Ophelia-like, too flowery, too lilies-in-the-pond. Hanging was too medieval, and he would need to soap the rope, and his face would turn blue, and his tongue would stick out disgustingly. Poisoning required scientific knowledge and would result in vomiting and shitting himself. Suicide by cop seemed like a good option since it wasn't quite strictly suicide, but Piotr was afraid of cops even in death, and they had a tendency to mess things up.

So he just hugged the pole, a koala,—no, a Russian bear transported against his will—unable and unwilling to move on. The crowd ignored him, and he ignored the crowd.

He spent his fiftieth birthday the night before cursing his fate in heavily accented English, drinking stale Diet Coke mixed with a few drops of leftover vodka, munching on his last Triscuit, and watching Mel Brooks' "The Twelve Chairs" on a scratched-up DVD lent to him by his neighbor, on a TV with a red stripe running continuously across the screen. Piotr's English wasn't up to the task because he had just recently arrived in the country, and because he hated foreign languages, but he knew the storyline by heart. It was so similar to his that his soul ached, coiled and uncoiled.

And then the landlord came and told him either to pay the two-month rent, all 1800 dollars of it, or vacate the room the next day. Piotr replied that he had no money, but will have some soon, very, very much money and that he was an honest gentleman. He wanted to add if his English would allow him, that the room had no promised AC but a lot of non-promised roaches, and that morbid fascination with the money was not becoming of a decent human being, and that all those problems justify a hefty discount. The landlord cut him off by saying that he's heard this story before, a million times. Piotr wanted to offer his TV and the DVD as a partial payment, but the landlord said that he didn't know what the DVD was, repeated his warning, and left.

Now, hanging on to the light pole in the most Russian-American corner of the globe, Piotr heard the voice of his stomach. It spoke loudly and shamelessly, and it didn't care about anything else but food. Then he saw the sign.

It was almost in his native language: *"turkey sandvich one dolar i 99 centov,"* and it sang to him from across the street like a siren from a Greek myth. $1.99, he still could afford that. He might even have two *sandviches.*

Piotr put the suicide thoughts aside, let go of the pole, and stepped onto the pavement.

Mark Budman

Two heartbeats later, he heard a loud hissing. Piotr turned his head—his vertebrae made a grinding sound—and saw a giant beast, a green reptile, an angry downtown deity gaining on him. Something that seemed like the object of his quest, his soul's lust, his lost pearls, his Ziggurat, shone on the deity's slanted forehead, firing the sun's reflection into Piotr's eyes. Another mirage? Impossible! Piotr leaned forward to catch his treasure.

A strong hand grabbed the collar of his tweed jacket and pulled him back to the sidewalk. The top button of Piotr's shirt popped off and his tie was tightened uncomfortably. He lost his breath and the ability to reason.

"Easy, buddy," a pleasant feminine voice said in English, in an accent that Piotr instantly recognized. "Watch the traffic."

Instead of a deity, a car with a diamond-shaped hood ornament idled a foot or two away from them, and a teenage driver in a tilted baseball cap with the logo "Make America Great Again" was shouting obscenities at Piotr. Truly, another mirage and a disastrously American one at that.

Piotr imagined his body shoved into an ambulance, dead on arrival at the hospital, and then lying, even thinner and paler than usual, in a casket made of fake wood. He hugged himself with both hands as if he had already been dumped into the grave. No, he wasn't ready to die, after all. Piotr's leg refused to hold him. He would have dropped to the pavement if not for the stranger's hand.

The woman was almost as tall as Piotr, perhaps a hundred eighty centimeters, or, speaking in American terms, five-eleven, but more muscular, with the skin the color of cream with a few drops of blood, and short black hair that stuck to her face of a thirty-something elf. Her green eyes seemed to extract Piotr's brain from his skull for careful examination. A diamond stud pierced her left ear. She oozed the charisma of a Hollywood star, a popular politician, or a used car salesman of the month. Some would call it animal magnetism. Russians called it *simpatichnaya*.

"I'm grateful to you for saving my life, young lady," Piotr managed to say. He wished to leave, but he had no place to go. Except for the *sandvich* place, which had lost its appeal suddenly.

"How grateful?"

"Pardon me?"

"My favorite type of gratitude is money. Every other type is open to interpretation."

A train passing on the rails above the street drowned out his last words. Then a thunderclap engulfed even that sound. The rain came down in streams of barely diluted acid. Piotr didn't know how to react. Though he didn't face a hulking man, Piotr was reasonably sure that Brooklyn was full of innocent-looking, charismatic female robbers, kidnappers, and scam artists. He had to be careful. A gypsy had told him once that he would have a long life, but Piotr never trusted foreigners.

"Don't be alarmed, milord," the woman said now with a disarming smile. "I'd settle for you buying me lunch. No *sandvich* places, please. A real restaurant."

Buying? A real restaurant? She obviously couldn't be aware of the catastrophic state of Piotr's finances. But the falling rain was forcing Piotr to make up his mind.

Cutting through the crowd of sad-eyed Russian men in woolen caps, plump women slathered in makeup, and crew-cut hoodlums shielded by leather jackets, Piotr and his rescuer walked the steaming asphalt of the Brighton Beach sidewalk. Roller-blading teenagers in torn jeans zoomed by.

They passed by the entrance of the *apteka*, a pharmacy, which advertised emu oil, remote psychic healing (bring a recent photograph of a patient), and Canadian drugs. They

passed by the window of a shoe boutique, with its manne-
quins clad in metallic sandals, leather mules, and nothing
else. They passed by a video store displaying a poster of a
Russian actress in a bikini and a space helmet, her crimson
fingernails tight around the long barrel of a ray gun.

By the time they entered Odessa Mama, Piotr was
soaked, but his savior seemed to repel the rainwater. The
air-conditioning hummed asthmatically and music blared
in their native tongue. There was a familiar aroma of stale
tobacco smoke, sour cabbage, and spilled alcohol. Photo-
graphs of a man with the rosy face of an aging piglet posing
with various dignitaries adorned the walls. The wall under the
photograph next to Piotr's table was dented. *A bullet hole?* He
didn't care anymore.

The waitress, a big Russian *baba*, approached and
stood by with her hands folded on her chest. As Piotr and his
new acquaintance checked the menu, her lips stretched into
the resigned smile of a below-minimum-wage employee.

They ordered and the waitress left the table. Piotr
followed the movements of her thick hips with his eyes, more
from instinct than desire.

"I'm Penelopa Belkina," the savior said. "The Americans spell my first name with the E on the end. As you can
tell, my father liked Homer. And you are?"

"I'm Piotr Osipovich Voronin," Piotr said, separating
his bottom from the sticky vinyl seat of the chair—forcing
it to emit a sound halfway between a moan and breaking
wind—and bowing. He didn't offer his hand, because he was
taught that a woman has to offer her hand first. Instead, he
adjusted the tie he had bought on his arrival in America to
blend in with the native crowd. Besides, any stranger's hands
were most probably unclean. Then he realized that Penelopa
had already touched him. In the pocket of his jacket, Piotr
had a bottle of tea tree oil, a potent germ killer, and he would

apply it to his hand liberally as soon as possible.

"Still using patronymics, Piotr Osipovich? How long have you been in this country?"

"Seven months and three days." Piotr leaned back and scratched his carefully combed brown-gray hair. He had only one hundred thirty dollars and a few rubles in his pocket, his entire capital, and he wasn't eager to part with a single penny or kopeck. Yet a gentleman had to do what a gentleman had to do. Stepping off the path of reciprocal altruism was worse than poverty and death.

"Ah, a veteran. I've only been here for half a year. How is your English?"

Piotr smiled politely. Around Brighton, one could easily get by with only a few English words, but Piotr knew several hundred, and generally wasn't hesitant to string them together in front of a native speaker. It helped that many words had crept into the lexicon of New Russia in the last twenty years: "bucks," "killer," "weekend," "show," "fitness," "stylist," "image-maker," "login" and "hacker." Still, this Penelopa spoke better English than he did.

"So, what are you doing in this citadel of liberty?" Penelopa continued, leaning toward Piotr. "Pursuing the American dream? It's a moving target. Hard to catch. Unless you are a part of the elite."

It would be so foolish to tell his secret to this perfect stranger. Piotr could be called many things, but a fool wasn't one of them. That's what the same shifty gypsy had told him. Piotr could have said that everyone's dream is different, or that he was too practical for dreaming, or that he already caught his dream. But he needed help.

His money and options were running out. He had no one to turn to. His only confidante, his aunt, was dead, and he had no friends on this side of the ocean. Women didn't like him anymore. In fact, they never had. So, it was either tell-

Mark Budman

ing the truth to this perfect stranger or perhaps crossing the street again, this time with his eyes closed.

Piotr scanned the dining room to make sure that no spy was hiding under the dirty tablecloths. Satisfied, he leaned toward Penelopa and whispered, choosing the words carefully. "I'm searching for a treasure. Pearls."

Penelopa's eyes sparkled. "Ah, treasure! I love treasure stories."

"My relative had family pearls of great value; she called them the Ziggurats. When she decided to emigrate to America, she feared that the Russian customs authorities wouldn't let her take them with her."

The waitress brought two plates of grayish chicken, surrounded by a few shreds of cheerless lettuce and tomatoes, a cut loaf of dark bread, and a bottle of wine from the Caucasian Mountains, which to a Russian was like the French wine to an American.

When she left, Piotr gulped down a glass of wine and studied Penelopa's face. If this woman were a bird, she would fly at the front of the V-formation, or at least create the impression that her task was the hardest.

Piotr felt woozy from the alcohol he so rarely drank. But he steamed ahead. "My relative had a set of homemade pillows she had inherited from her grandmother. Seven of them. She stuffed the pearls in one and mailed it all to the post office in New York so the Russian authorities would not confiscate the pearls. She even insured them for $500, all she could afford. But then she died the day before getting on the plane. A heart attack, happens in my family. At that time, I had only been here for 53 days. I knew no English. I had no idea what to do, whom to contact. By the time I turned around, the post office had sold the things at auction. The pillows turned out to have their own value. Who would have thought?"

"How much are these Ziggurats worth?"

"Who knows? They are perfect quality, and there are seven."

"Seven!" Penelopa's eyes shone. "Spectacular! So, you want to be rich, huh?"

Piotr thought about the answer. Should he tell the truth to the fabulously energetic Penelopa? Should he tell her that the most important branch of the United States government—its immigration arm, ICE, U.S. Immigration and Customs Enforcement—was going to deport him unless he found a good lawyer in less than a month? Should he tell her that he didn't always think about the Ziggurats, but only when he was awake? Should he tell her that he longed to touch the Ziggurats one more time, to feel again their magic and invigorating presence? Should he tell her that he was the last descendant of a Russian noble family, left penniless on the streets of New York and that selling this heirloom was the only way for him to climb back up the social ladder, to the place where he belonged? Should he tell her that it would be criminal if someone else should find the pearls and enjoy them? Should he tell her about his suicidal thoughts? Should he tell her that he was in such dire straits that even a bucket of tea tree oil couldn't cleanse him?

"Yes," he said. "I want to be rich."

"A very noble goal. We are alike, you and I. We are the poets of life."

Piotr nodded. He was a poet. His tongue lusted after a few well-connected words the way his loins longed for female flesh.

"I assume the pearls can't be felt inside the pillow?" Penelopa said. It seemed like she could switch subjects faster than a government spokeswoman. "No strange lumps pinching your neck?"

"I guess so."

"You said that the post office sold the pillows at an auction?"

"Right."

"What was the name of the auction house?" Penelopa asked.

"AAA Empire Auctions."

"A very imaginative name... Do you know who bought them?"

"I asked. They said it was confidential."

"Nothing's confidential for Penelopa. I'll hack their website. Easy."

"I can't pay anything upfront, but if you help me find the pearls, I'll pay you most generously. How does that sound?"

Penelopa cut off a piece of chicken. Piotr watched her chew with the fascination of a boy on his first trip to a zoo, watching a panther devouring a deer.

"It sounds good," Penelopa said when she finished chewing. "I like generous payments. But let's talk like business people. Are you a businessman?"

Piotr nodded. Of course, he was a businessman. Wasn't it obvious?

"We will split the cost fifty-fifty," Penelopa said. "I'm sure that sounds good to you."

Piotr got up. Now, he would show the panther who was the businessman here. "Fifty-fifty? You are insulting me, young lady."

"Look at this. We've got an alpha male here. My teeth are chattering." Penelopa pointed at Piotr with another piece of chicken, skewered by a fork, and then deposited it into her mouth.

Piotr checked around. The waitress from across the room watched him with a smirk. Piotr's chest deflated. He sat down. He felt dizzy and nauseous. He had to check his blood pressure.

"OK, OK," Penelopa said. "I see you are in distress. I don't want to cause you any hardship. I'll take 45 percent. Deal?"

Piotr's mind parsed the words carefully. He knew he had to surrender, but to part with 45 percent of something, even if he didn't have that something, was unbearably hard.

"Deal," he whispered and closed his eyes. He had crossed his Rubicon, and his fate rested in the hands of a woman he just met.

#

"When do we start?" Penelopa asked half an hour later after Piotr reluctantly shelled out forty-two dollars and eleven cents for the restaurant bill and tips.

"I don't know," Piotr said. The acids generated by the meal were already rising in his throat.

"How about starting now? Do you have a computer at home?"

Piotr lowered his gaze.

"Don't worry," Penelopa said, "I don't want to invade your privacy. Let's go to my place."

Penelopa's apartment was a Spartan affair—one bedroom, a tiny kitchen, a living room with a computer and a framed photograph on a small table, and two plastic chairs. It felt like a half-star hotel room, except that it smelled of dollar-store perfume instead of disinfectants. Yet it was located just one block from the ocean—a prime area for the denizens of this neighborhood, former inhabitants of the Russian port of Odessa, the pearl of the Black Sea.

"I don't have a place anymore," Piotr said. "I have no wife. My landlord evicted me. I'm running out of funds."

Penelopa pushed her hair away from her face. "You know what," she said, slapping Piotr on the shoulder. "You can stay here for a few days. My boyfriend won't be back until next Sunday. I'll give you a cot and clean sheets. You could sleep in the living room as long as you don't snore. Use my toothpaste. But don't get any ideas. I have a black belt in Tae Kwon Do. If you enter my room, you're dead. But I'll cut off your limp cock and stuff it in your mouth before you die."

"I don't snore," Piotr said and wiped a single tear with a lace handkerchief, his auntie's gift. "You are too kind. I'll pay you back all the rent when we sell the Ziggurats. That plus ten percent interest. The word of a gentleman."

Penelopa gestured dismissively. "Don't worry. I'll just take another twenty percent of the Ziggurats."

When she left for her room, Piotr examined the photograph in the bright city light steaming from the windows. It showed Penelopa embracing a tall light-haired man. The man's smile seemed strained, and Piotr thought he detected a badly Photoshopped black eye on his face.

Piotr couldn't fall asleep. There was no AC. He lay sweating on the cot between the sheets of questionable cleanness and cursed himself for sharing his secret with this dangerous woman. All was ruined now. That was obvious. Penelopa would find the pillow and take the treasure for herself. 100% of it. She was too quick and too ruthless. An elite con woman. It was as clear as day. She would take it and discard Piotr. Maybe even kill him, finishing off his Odyssey? Strangle him with her bare hands. He didn't want to die anymore. Death was for losers.

Where were Piotr's eyes? Why couldn't he see it coming? Where was his head? Why couldn't he think straight? Was he a fool after all?

What should he do? He couldn't go on living without the Ziggurats. Escaping would be useless. He had to act. His cause was just.

He got up, stood on wobbly legs for a few minutes, and then paced the room, biting his fingernails. He rummaged through the kitchen cabinet, found a carving knife, and weighed it in his hands. Heavy. He probed its tip with his finger. Sharp. On his tiptoes, he came to the closed door of the bedroom.

This woman's just a crook, he thought. No one will mourn her. Not even her boyfriend. In fact, I will do society a favor. I'm like a deputized cop now.

He opened the door wide enough to stick his head into the opening. It was also hot here. Penelopa lay supine in semi-darkness, snoring lightly. Her sheet slipped down, exposing her round and succulent breasts. Her pillow fell on the floor. Piotr felt a stirring in his loins but it subsided quickly.

"A ruffled mind makes a restless pillow," he thought. Charlotte Bronte?

Never mind her womanhood. She's a female snake. One good swing and it's over. A shiny arc of vengeance and justice. Vengeance and justice are never foolish.

Piotr pushed the door more and the hinges protested. Penelopa stirred and Piotr froze. At the same moment, a siren wailed outside, squeezing Piotr's heart with its heavy paw. He imagined Penelopa jumping at him, her lovely breasts bouncing, her eyes throwing thunderbolts, steam coming from her mouth, her hands locking at his throat.

A measure of time passed, shorter than eternity but too long for comfort. Seeing that Penelopa didn't react, Piotr made a tiny step forward. He was a Raskolnikov and Penelopa was a pawnbroker. He made another step.

Steel cuts flesh, he thought. Steel cuts arteries. He imagined Penelopa's snoring turning into a gargle of blood, and he instinctively raised his hand to his own throat.

Doubts be damned. Altruism be damned. Honor be damned. As soon as he would be done, every piece of broken glass on the streets of this city would turn into a pearl, and the morbidly fascinating strangers around him, both the

Mark Budman

locals and the Russians, would stop praying in their skyscraper-ziggurats for money and power over other people.

He, Piotr, would bring justice to the world, namely remove the oppressed common man like himself from under the thumb of the elite and con men, which were one and the same.

But at this moment, during this elusive moment when spring was turning into free fall, the American air dazzled and blinded him. He felt pressure in his chest, radiating into his jaw. Something exploded inside him, and he dropped the knife. Or maybe he thought he did. Maybe he still was holding it and cutting. He wasn't sure anymore. The air enveloped him and lifted him up, up, and up. Through the ceiling. Through the roof. Through the low clouds. Through the contrails of a jet. Through the orbits of satellites. Through the orbits of the alien ships observing the earth (unless they were angels). To the place where a lonely man who had lost everything needed neither pearls nor knives. To the place that had neither triumphs nor failures. To the place that required no quests for attainment, because all quests end there, either by accident or by design. Whatever it was, he would find out soon.

Stick Figures

The interpreter and his wife take turns with the twins. Their daughter and her husband are long at work.

The interpreter and his wife feed the kids together. Food flies all over. Tiny pieces of chicken. Zucchini. Home-made bread. Cheerios. He calls the room the mess hall.

The biggest discovery in his childhood was learning that English speakers used a different alphabet than the Russians. What a waste of memory cells.

The daughter and her husband come home. The interpreter is relieved of his duties until the morning. He watches Netflix on his computer. He prefers comedies and animation. They are less messy.

Later in the evening, in his bed, the interpreter listens to the howling of the wind. He's sympathetic. He would howl too if they would leave him outside in such weather.

He takes his laptop and writes a story set in the

Mark Budman

spring. Because he knows that spring will come:

I walk the pair of two-and-a-half-year-old identical twins outside my daughter's house. They collect pet rocks, grass clippings, wildflowers, last year's pine needles, and give them to their *Deda* for safekeeping. *Deda* means grandfather in Russian. *Deda* is me. *Deda* is old by definition. I meet it: I'm older than the surrounding hills by a factor of three.

One of the twins called me a *translator* today. No one calls me that, or at least no one should because I'm a medical interpreter and not a translator, and there is no one around with such a profession. Not in any books we read for them, and they are not watching TV. A mystery.

"Why do you call me that?" I asked.

She changed the subject to her dolls.

"How old are you?" I ask her now.

She brings up her large gray eyes. She points two fingers and then bends one more. "Two and one half."

She is smart. Took after me.

"Great job. And how old am I? Guess."

She struggles. It must be a big number.

"Four, five, six?"

"Six," she says.

"Not quite right."

When I was four, we lived in Siberia.

When I was five, we moved to Kazakhstan.

When I was six, we moved again, to Moldova.

Not because we liked to travel, but because Stalin exiled my family. Since then I moved a lot, crossing borders and the ocean, finding a new home at least a dozen times.

Now, I interpret for money, pleasure, and the good of the country. Now, I help to raise my grandkids for the benefit of the whole of mankind.

The other twin gives me yet another pet rock. It's

warm to the touch, and it looks like a miniature meteorite. It's identical to one of its earlier collected sisters. Like a meteorite, it traveled far, had time for reflection, and is probably even older than me. By a factor of six.

I collect the girls, and we are heading home. Home is where the twins are.

The interpreter turns off his laptop and falls asleep. He dreams about the world inhabited by orange and purple stick figures with pretty hair who eat very neatly and never howl. There are no maladies in this world, no guns, and everyone has anything they need, and there is only one language so that he can quit his paying job. He likes that. He's good at drawing and solving puzzles. They won't fire him from this job. He smiles in his sleep. He has just solved all the world's problems without firing a single bullet from his stick gun.

Mark Budman

Ponce de Leon's
Baby Breath

The two-year-old twins stand on two-step stools by the window, observing the neighborhood. Inquisitive face, mismatching outfits, matching stools, double-pane glass, and, behind it, a dangerously disorganized universe.

The interpreter of dreams and afflictions, their grandfather, or *Deda* in Russian, sits on the floor behind them, checking the news on his smartphone. The news is grim. Fires, assassinations, accidents, hurricanes, floods, wars, diseases, bear markets, terrorism, and polarizing tweets. He's the first bastion in the twin's protection.

Funny, but "*Deda*" is an anagram of "dead."

Deda is aware of that. He wants to find the youth elixir. Not that he desires to be young again for selfish reasons; he doesn't trust the young any longer. They're too egotistic, think too much about sex, and are easily manipulated. They have no respect for their elders. They don't even know what "respect" and "elders" mean.

The other day, at Walmart, a young cable company salesman was trying to pitch him something or other.

"I've already heard your pitch," *Deda* said because he did.

"Peach? We are not selling peaches here."

A typical youngster. A jerk. Making fun of immigrants and old men.

Deda wants to help his granddaughters for a long time. He wants to protect them and to teach them. He has to be young for that. He searches for the answer. But everything he finds on Google is either cons or unproven speculations or too far into the future. Stem cell brain implants, senescent cells elimination, sirtuin protein Sirt1...

"Neighbor," the twins shout, "neighbor. Man, man."

When they say "man," it means they're afraid. They don't call old guys like *Deda* men.

Deda rises to investigate. He still can do it without holding on to the furniture. But he's running out of time. He ambulates to the window.

The neighbor is getting into his SUV. The twins jump up and down and shriek. *Deda* should tweet it to the world, or at least to his 2,245 followers. The twins don't like this neighbor. Maybe because he speaks with an accent? But so does *Deda*. Probably because the neighbor's large and young.

Today, *Deda* finds something potentially promising on Amazon. A potion, a mixture of herbs from the Himalayas, the stem cells from the ancient insects trapped in amber, and powdered shells from the Sea of Reeds. They call it Ponce de Leon's Baby Breath. How quaint. The reviews are ecstatic, with "before" and "after" pics. They show trim, erect middle-aged men and women, and slouched sour-faced millennials. Funny, the potion comes with its reverse pill. The eternal youth with a 30-days guarantee.

But the interpreter's wife, the grandmother, shouts

Mark Budman

that they need to take the twins outside. The four of them walk in pairs, holding hands. Once they cross the street into a meadow, the twins collect wildflowers, pulling them out with the roots. Whenever they go outside, the young flowers whisper to each other: "Hide! The twins are coming." Even the old grass clippings and yellow pine needles are not safe.

Back in the house, one of the twins finds a quiet moment for herself to climb into an easy chair and to read the *Cute Doggie Encyclopedia*. The other plays with the Young Doctor Kit.

Deda goes back to Ponce de Leon's Baby Breath. It's only $19.99 for twenty pills. The reverse pill is thrown in as a free gift. One pill a day, and if you won't be younger in a month, you can get your money back, minus $4.99 for the shipping. They don't specify how to measure the getting younger process. He guesses it might be self-evident.

He's 80% sure it's a con. He orders it anyway and then it's time to help his wife to feed the twins. He doesn't tell her about the order. He'll try it on himself first. Meanwhile, he's teaching the twins Russian.

"Pillow" is "*poduhska*."

"No," one of them says.

"No? What is it, then?"

"Pillow."

A week later, the package arrives.

He's tempted to open it now but eats first. Veggies: black-eyed peas, brown rice, white mushrooms, olive oil. No salt, no spices. Why did they call it black-eyed? Who gave such tiny creatures a black eye?

In the evening, *Deda* locks himself in the bathroom and opens the jar. The pills look like 81 mg aspirin he takes daily except that they have a faint flowery scent. Lavender? Very soothing.

He takes one with a glass of water. Nothing happens.

He has to give it time to work. He goes to bed. He hits the *podushka* but it takes him a while to fall asleep. Lavender? Very soothing.

Twenty days later, he's on his last pill. He feels no difference. He looks the same. He thinks the same. He's the same. It was a con. He has to apply for a refund. He lost a hard-earned $4.99.

The next morning, he wakes up in the empty bed, with an erection. His wife is already up. He washes his face, half asleep.

He needs to go downstairs, to help take care of the twins, but he doesn't feel like it. He worked enough. Let his wife do it. He goes back to bed and unlocks his phone. He wants to check the news but ends up with some sexy lingerie ads. He forgot how curvy young women can be.

His wife calls from downstairs. He goes down reluctantly. Why is it always him? The brats have their parents after all. He's just a granddad. How many granddads take care of their grandkids? That's right. One. Just him. Funny, he doesn't feel like an old fart.

While he's walking down the staircase, something dawns on him. His thoughts are simple, childish even. He's full of energy. His muscles are tightly wound springs. What if he has already become young again? What if his wife looks at him with her mouth opened? What if the twins' faces get frozen? What if they point fingers and shout, "Man, man!" What if he becomes sour-faced, obnoxious, and entitled? Would he sit in the basement from now on, watching porn and smoking weed?

He turns and runs up the stairs, skipping every other step. He's afraid to look into the mirror. He searches for the reverse pill. Funny, he saw it before but never noticed it has a crude picture of a sticking tongue on it. To hell with the anagrams. To hell with the unchecked erections. To hell with

Mark Budman

youth. To hell with death. He swallows the pill dry while he still has his resolve, and breathes in and out, suddenly happy like a boy of two.

Penelopa in her Cute Leatherstockings

Penelopa's father was teaching ancient history at a local college, in the Soviet city of Odessa, and she hated him for giving her this pretentious name. And she hated all things ancient, as well as history, teachers, and colleges. It was hard to make a nickname out of Penelopa, and every other Russian- or Ukrainian-speaking child had several. Penny or Pippa had no meaning in Russian, and Poppa sounded like "ass."

In the height of the summer when she turned twelve, Penelopa sat on a low branch of a mulberry tree back at home, a slingshot in her belt, kissing a boy named Vanya. He was a better kisser than her friend Marina; Marina's kisses were sloppy. No wonder. Vanya was two years older than they were. But when Vanya put his hand between Penelopa's legs and tried to force them apart, she pushed him off the branch.

"Bitch," he yelled, lying flat on the soft ground. "Fuck you."

That wasn't fair. Even if she had already kissed two

people, she wasn't a bitch. Marina said that a real bitch kisses at least five people and lets at least one touch her down there. She didn't say if they have to do it all at once or one at a time.

Vanya knew nothing, and he was an asshole. She knew how to treat his kind. She pulled out her slingshot and loaded it with a round stone. She had full pockets of those and the neighborhood sparrows knew that.

She could've easily hit Vanya between the eyes, but she aimed at his chest. That was enough. He limped away. From that point on, she always carried a weapon.

Armed, she would run around with the boys and kick their asses when they made fun of her name. She could do everything better than they could, except for one thing. The boys would line up on the second floor of a condemned apartment building and pee, aiming at the circle they had drawn on the asphalt with chalk. And she just stood behind.

But a few years later, she could con them all.

She came to America, from the now independent country of Ukraine, by winning what they called a diversity immigrant visa. She was as diverse as they come: with a good measure of Russian, Ukrainian, Jewish, and Greek blood. If she had her own flag reflecting her background, it would be too busy.

Soon after arrival, shortly after she conned her first American, out of $1,056, she discovered a female urination device called GoGirl. She ordered two, went to a forest, made sure no one was around, drew a circle with her knife, climbed up a tree, aimed, and shot. Bingo. Now she took away the last advantage men had.

When she met Piotr, she pitied him and took him under her wing. There was a vulnerability about him, and she knew he was a nobleman deep inside. Too deep for most people to notice but she had an eagle eye.

Since Penelopa was always on a move, she didn't have a stable boyfriend. Picking men at the bar seemed dangerous. Though she was strong, a strange man could still overpower her, even if she really had a black belt in Tae Kwon Do, which she didn't.

One romantic night, Penelopa, dressed only in a garter belt and silk stockings, descended on sleeping Piotr just before dawn. She woke him up by covering his mouth with a kiss. He was both eager and gentle, but the foreplay lasted less than five minutes, and the main act was not even half of that. She didn't blame him; he tried. He even apologized. Twice. Once for each part of the act.

I should give him the benefit of the doubt, she thought. But then she decided she had sacrificed enough. He might grow too cocky. She left without saying a word, the sway of her hips signaling her disdain, and, back in her room, fell on her sword, er, vibrator.

She slept and had sex with Superman. It was great for a few super short minutes, until he had premature ejaculation and smothered her in his cum, green and shiny like the kryptonite.

"Nothing happened last night," she told Piotr in the morning. "You just had a wet dream. Don't get any ideas."

She turned away and then turned back sharply, expecting him to flip her a bird while she wasn't watching, but he didn't. She liked that.

The day they drove to the next pillow owner, after discarding the first three, she sat at the wheel, singing *Three Tankmen,* a Russian song that was way older than even Piotr.

Piotr rode shotgun, keeping one of the empty pillows under his lower back. He tried to sing along at first, but gave up and was watching the Upstate New York countryside instead. The clear air and unmolested forests showed no sign of

Mark Budman

American capitalists ruining the environment, as they used to claim in the old Soviet Union.

"How do you like Fennimore Cooperson's land?" Penelopa said. "They call it the Leatherstocking region."

"Fennimore Cooper," Piotr said automatically.

"Stop correcting me, or I'll make you pay for gas."

"It's Cooper anyway," Piotr said. "Not Cooperson. But I will be quiet from now on since my freedom of expression is worth nothing to you. This conversation is pointless anyway."

"It seems pointed to me."

"Ah, be quiet!"

"OK. I will sing *Katyusha*, then."

Two minutes later, when Penelopa finished with *Katyusha*, Piotr asked, "What is her name?"

"Whose name?"

"The woman you just hacked? The fourth pillow owner?"

"Precious. Isn't it precious?"

He laughed.

"It's not a laughing matter," Penelopa said. "She might be armed. Americans love their guns. Especially here, Upstate."

"Why aren't you armed?"

"I am. I'm armed with my brain. And I have a knife."

Piotr fell asleep shortly, and dreamed about Penelopa, dressed in leather stockings, shooting rays from her eyes at that woman Precious who was armed with two shotguns, an AR-15 assault rifle, a revolver, and a grenade launcher.

When he awoke, he told Penelopa about his dream.

"Do you want me to interpret it?"

"Go right ahead."

"It's your suppressed sexuality," she said. "You need to find your true love."

"You are my true love."

You and the pearls, he thought.

She smiled. "Oh, Piotr. Only if your actions match your words."

"Does it mean you want me to drive?"

"No, thanks."

She's young, Piotr thought. *Young people will die long after me just because they were born later. An unfair trick of nature.*

A young deer stood by the road, watching them, wearing leather from head to toe. Piotr waved but the deer didn't wave back.

Americans. You got to love them, even if they are young and wear leather all over.

The Most Excellent Immigrant

*There is a legend about a bird which sings just once in its life,
more sweetly than any other creature on the face of the earth.*
– Colleen McCullough, *The Thorn Birds*

The interpreter's half-pleasant nap is interrupted by the distinct pop-pop of automatic gunfire and shouts coming from above. The sounds don't come from heaven but the first floor of the American Civic Association immigration center. The interpreter is sitting in the basement at a donated kitchen table where he was supposed to translate some documents for the newly arrived immigrants. Some documents are medical, some not. It's a repetitive and thankless task. But he's a volunteer and therefore he takes it easy.

Most immigrants here, in Binghamton, NY, came from the former Soviet Union as refugees from the Nieces and Nephews of the Savior persecuted church and are Russian speakers. There are a few Latinos, Asians, and Africans, too.

The interpreter knows only Russian, and he picked up a bit of English over time. Or so he modestly says.

Just a short time ago, he had closed his eyes and the room floated. The junk furniture was gone. The interpreter faced Joseph, his ethereal mentor, across the marble conference table. There was a blood-red vase full of thistles and thorns, and two bottles of Evian.

Joseph and the interpreter were talking in the language of dreams. Two immigrants, they both climbed high in their adopted countries: at the peak of their respected careers the interpreter became a program manager at IBM, and Joseph was the viceroy of ancient Egypt, second only to the Pharaoh.

"We need our adoptive country, it's obvious," the interpreter said. "Otherwise, we would have stayed home. But does the country need us? We have to be careful. The immigrant is like a physician: *primum non nocere*, "first, do no harm.""

"Some of us saved our new country from hunger," Joseph said. He wore a business suit and tie. He had never worn that getup before. "And don't show off your Latin or I'll talk in *r n km.t.*"

The interpreter nodded. He wasn't that proficient in ancient Egyptian. "Some natives would say it's better to be hungry than to have immigrants descending on us like a locust. Some natives say that the immigrants reject the values of the land. So we must be not just good but excellent. The most excellent."

Joseph takes a sip of Evian. "You said values? What values do you have in your country? Buying guns and eating hamburgers? We haven't had either in Egypt and did fine for many thousand years."

"Nothing's wrong with guns. We, immigrants, should be able to protect ourselves."

Mark Budman

Actually, the interpreter has never seen an immigrant with a gun. He shot an AK-47 when was conscripted into the Soviet Army, but it was many years ago.

Joseph got up. "The thornbird is about to sing, the last time in his life. Listen carefully." And he was gone. And the gunfire and the shots had begun.

The interpreter is quick. He barricades the door as quietly as he can and hides in a closet. But then he thinks of others upstairs. He wasn't serving in the army for nothing. He's got to be the most excellent immigrant even if he has to pay the price. He searches the room. No AR-15s or even AK-47s. He grabs the most American weapon he can find—a baseball bat.

He climbs up the stairs. His legs are cotton balls under him. He wants to pee. He's the most unlikely hero that has ever come to this country.

When he is on the top step, the shouting and gun-shots stop. The death song stops. Only the sirens are still singing outside.

The floor is littered with dead bodies and covered with blood. He can't tell if they are immigrants or natives. Except for an older woman, a volunteer English teacher.

He sees a dead man wearing a bullet-proof vest and a bright green nylon jacket, with two pistols next to him. There is a hole in his head. His face is contorted in the last grimace of pain he will ever have in this world. He will never be young again.

Since no cops are here, and since no one else has fire-arms, the man must have killed himself. The interpreter rec-ognizes him, though he's not Russian but from East Asia. The man just lost his engineering job at IBM, and he spoke bad English and the natives teased him. Enough to get depressed. Enough to dream of protecting himself. Enough to fail at his dream. Because even the strongest of us snap under pressure.

Unless he wanted to improve this new country by showing the evil of firearms? Or, on the contrary, their necessity for protection of the weak? Or maybe he wanted to emphasize that death treats everyone equally, natives and immigrants alike?

How else could the interpreter interpret such an act? The interpreter's legs buckle. He sits on the floor and watches the man whose spread arms remind him of a dead bird. The thornbird sang his song. It had no words but only action. If it had words, it would run mostly in capital letters, bad English notwithstanding, and began with "THE FiRST I WANT TO SAY SORRY."

It was the best he could do. *For the best is only bought at the cost of great pain.*

Mark Budman

A Love Story in the Time of a Blizzard

The old man sleeps alone.

The old man sleeps alone, though he is married.

The old man sleeps alone, though he is married, and his wife is healthy and at home.

The old man sleeps alone, though he is married, and his wife is healthy and at home, and they love each other more than ever.

The old man sleeps alone, though he is married, and his wife is healthy and at home, and they love each other more than ever, and can't be without each other for long.

***

The old man's wife is not alone.

The old man's wife is not alone, and she sleeps in a different room.

The old man's wife is not alone, and she sleeps in a different room next to two more people.

The old man's wife is not alone, and she sleeps in a

different room next to two more people, and she loves both.

The old man's wife is not alone, and she sleeps in a different room next to two more people, and she loves both, but they don't love her yet, though they surely will one day, because everyone else does.

***

The old man's wife once said sex is dirty.

The old man's wife once said sex is dirty, and she meant that at the time.

The old man's wife once said sex is dirty, and she meant that at the time, but she never says that now.

The old man's wife once said sex is dirty, and she meant that at the time, but she never says that now, and allows some infrequent sex.

The old man's wife once said sex is dirty, and she meant that at the time, but she never says that now, and allows some infrequent sex after which she bathes for hours and washes everything.

***

The old man is not banished.

The old man is not banished, but he chose to sleep alone.

The old man is not banished, but he chose to sleep alone because he's not good with babies.

The old man is not banished, but he chose to sleep alone because he's not good with babies, and that's what his wife says.

***

The old man's wife is a great nanny.

The old man's wife is a great nanny for the premature twins.

The old man's wife is a great nanny for the premature twins who are their grandkids.

The old man's wife is a great nanny for the premature

Mark Budman

twins who are their grandkids and whose busy parents work hard.

***

Both grandkids were born two months too early and spent these two months in the neonatal intensive care unit. The kids who can function on their own and leave the unit are called graduates. The grandkids graduated with honors.

***

It's not easy to become an old man.

It's not easy to become an old man since it takes time, and your path is littered with burst rosy bubbles and broken clocks.

It's not easy to become an old man since it takes time, and your path is littered with burst rosy bubbles and broken clocks, but, on the other hand, it's automatic.

It's not easy to become an old man since it takes time, and your path is littered with burst rosy bubbles and broken clocks, but, on the other hand, it's automatic, and young people would give up their seats for you in the public transport.

***

The old man's wife has help.

The old man's wife has help, a young woman who speaks English and Spanish.

The old man's wife has help, a young woman who speaks English and Spanish, but who was born in this country.

The old man's wife has help, a young woman who speaks English and Spanish, but who was born in this country, and who teaches the old man Spanish when the babies are asleep.

***

Someone enters the old man's room at night while a blizzard is raging outside, and the snow falls black with soot.

Someone enters the old man's room at night, while a blizzard is raging outside, and the snow falls black with soot, and he sees it's a naked woman.

Someone enters the old man's room at night, while a blizzard is raging outside, and the snow falls black with soot, and he sees it's a naked woman and it's his wife.

Someone enters the old man's room at night, while a blizzard is raging outside, and the snow falls black with soot, and he sees it's a naked woman, and it's his wife, and he's not sure if he isn't still dreaming.

***

The old man came from Russia.

The old man came from Russia, but he speaks English well, for a foreigner.

The old man came from Russia but he speaks English well, for a foreigner, and writes in that language even better.

The old man came from Russia but he speaks English well, for a foreigner, and writes in that language even better, and he dreams that someone will compare him to Nabokov.

***

In some languages, the word *baba* is used when showing respect to an older man. In English, it can mean a small rich sponge cake, typically soaked in rum-flavored syrup. Very sweet.

In Russian *baba* is always a female. The old man is a language guru. An expert, authority, leading light, professional, master, pundit, buff, whiz, and connoisseur.

The old man works as a medical interpreter, serving Russian patients who speak little English. The other day he saw the nurses washing an old lady. They uncovered her in front of him when she soiled herself in her bed. The violation of medical ethics, and the best way of making a man impotent. He turned away quickly, but not quickly enough.

***

The babies call his wife *baba*.

The babies call his wife *baba*, and *baba* can be a de-

Mark Budman

rogatory word in Russian.

The babies call his wife *baba*, and *baba* can be a derogatory word in Russian unless it's a sweet grandmother.

The babies call his wife *baba*, and *baba* can be a derogatory word in Russian unless it's a sweet grandmother, but the old man's wife is an athletic, attractive woman and sometimes fierce.

***

The old man's wife climbs into his bed.

The old man's wife climbs into his bed and holds him tight.

The old man's wife climbs into his bed and holds him tight, but a baby cries in the next room.

The old man's wife climbs into his bed and holds him tight, but a baby cries in the next room, and the wife gets up, puts on her nightgown, and leaves.

***

Now, the old man's wife won't need to bathe for hours.

Now, the old man's wife won't need to bathe for hours and wash everything.

Now, the old man's wife won't need to bathe for hours and wash everything, and even the snow will fall clean.

Now, the old man's wife won't need to bathe for hours and wash everything, and even the snow will fall clean, but the old man feels dirty.

***

The old man comes to the window.

The old man comes to the window and watches the ice sheet forming over 10 inches of snow.

The old man comes to the window and watches the ice sheet forming over 10 inches of snow and writes a poem in three languages.

Soy un abuelito tierno,

And *baba* is my wife.
I am a sweet grandfather,
And I long for my wife.
Вот и сказочке конец,
а кто слушал—молодец.
And he could tell anyone willing to listen that
молодец is attaboy, but no one wants to listen to an old man.
***

The old man falls asleep and dreams that he walks with Nabokov through the blizzard, and reads him his poem and that the writer slaps him high, and then they ride in a one-horse open sleigh until the horse slips and falls, and breaks its leg, and Nabokov shoots it with a Russian Civil War pistol.

"It was an old horse," he says. "No one will fix it."

The old man wants to say that veterinarians can do wonders now, but he wakes up.

The old man wakes up cold and alone and with a taste of a dead horse in his mouth. He's happy he's alive and has a beautiful wife and grandkids. He's working on another poem. He'll write it in five languages, and it will rhyme, and he will publish it in *The New Yorker,* and his daughter, the twins' mother, will give him and his wife a night off.

The old man takes a long, cold shower as if it's his last one.

But it won't be. When they love you, you will live forever.

Mark Budman

John and Phillip

The two nutcrackers appeared the day after Thanksgiving. It was too early for Christmas and just about time for Hanukkah, but the owners were apparently impatient.

The nutcrackers stood by the door of the neighbor's house, taller than the interpreter's twin granddaughters, but shorter than his wife. The interpreter was sure he'd seen their pics before on social media. Twitter, perhaps? Whenever it was, they had a ton of likes and comments.

"What's their names?" one of the twins asked when they stopped to observe the nutcrackers.

The interpreter wanted to say Moses and Aaron but decided that this joke, if it were a joke, was too complicated for the two-and-half-year olds.

"John and Phillip," he said instead. "They are identical twins, like you. But they are boys."

"Why do they have big teeth?"

"To crack nuts. Luckily, they don't have nut allergies.

Imagine if they would."

The interpreter's daughter, the twins' mother, and her husband didn't let the twins have nuts. Choking hazard. The interpreter was horrified. He loved nuts more than chocolate. He couldn't imagine a happy life without them.

"Why crack?"

"Nuts have hard shells. But the seeds are yummy, yummy in my tummy."

"What is a shell?"

The other twin was watching her sister with her mouth open. That's sincere respect.

"A protective outer case," the interpreter said.

"What is a case? What is outer?"

At least they didn't ask what "protective" means. They knew that word. Their grandfather was their protector.

After nightfall, the interpreter went for a stroll, alone this time. His wife and daughter and the daughter's husband were busy as always. The interpreter stopped by Philip and John again. They hardly moved since he left them, and seemed to be impervious to the cold, though they had only a thin layer of paint to protect their bodies. Their smiles were wooden.

"By the looks of you, I suppose you don't frequent Twitter often, fellows," the interpreter said in Russian. They probably had the same chance of understanding him if he spoke in English or Swahili or just communicated telepathically. "Not as often as me, I suppose. Today, I received the most intelligent and well-researched reply to my Twitter post: WOW. Yes, the entire reply was only three letters. My post had one like, but that reply got thirty. Unbelievable. Don't you think so?"

John and Phillip didn't reply. Perhaps they failed their telepathic class. Perhaps they were banned from Twitter. Perhaps they resented Russian interference in American elections.

When he left, Philip, who stood on the right, turned to John.

"Another immigrant. There must be a nest somewhere."

"Come on," John said. "We are just off the boat ourselves. We might not look it, but we are Chinese immigrants."

"I feel like a native," Philip said. "I look like a native. If I walked, I'd walk like a native. So I must be a native. Just look at my off-white face and good-quality teeth. All immigrants have bad teeth."

"I have three million identical twins," John said. "How did I end up with a repugnican?"

"Demorat. Elitist."

In the evening, the interpreter helped his wife put the grandkids to bed.

"I'm scared," one of the twins said.

"Scared of what?"

"Of John and Phillip."

"How come?"

"They got big teeth."

"So?"

"What if they bite us?"

"Only if you are nuts. Are you nuts?"

"No."

"So you are safe."

The twins fell asleep eventually. Their arms and legs twitched. Perhaps they dreamed about John and Philip.

The interpreter waded into their dream, wearing a wooden smile, black jackboots, red coat with yellow piping, and red hat, and fed nuts to everyone, including John and Philip. The nutcrackers were pleased. They said, Wow. The kids were pleased. They said, "yummy, yummy in my tummy."

In a dream, you can do everything you want as long

as you protect the kids and be civil to your fellow immigrants and natives. That's how the interpreter interpreted dreaming. He was an expert, recognized by both political wings of humanity, and by natives and immigrants alike.

The Dream
Thieves' Cream

T hey are the dream thieves," the doctor said. "They steal
dreams from you and then resell them on the Dark Web
for Bitcoins. Impossible to trace."

The interpreter of dreams and afflictions contemplated that. He knew what the Dark Web was. He read the website called "How to Access Notorious Dark Web Anonymously
(10 Step Guide)." It was scary. The website itself knew his IP
address, his location, his browser, and screen resolution. And
that's even *before* he accessed the Dark Web. It seemed like it
moved across the river of time in both directions.

He came to the doctor because he couldn't sleep.
Even when he slept, he had nightmares. Exploding planets.
Falling planes. His grandchildren's babysitter bad-mouthing
the interpreter's fiction. He didn't know how to interpret
that.

"But is it a malady?" he asked the doctor.

Her eyebrows arched above her death-star eyes. She
turned away from him and began to type. "I'll prescribe you a

cream. Apply a small dollop to your forehead. I will also give you a sample."

"Would my insurance cover it?"

"You have to ask that in the front office."

Yesterday, the interpreter asked one of his identical twin grandchildren, a two-and half-year-old, "What do you want to be when you grow up?"

"A shot doctor."

Seeing that he doesn't understand, the girl brought a giant plastic syringe from the Young Doctor Kit.

Just about everyone on his wife's side was doctors: herself, her late parents, her sister, and one of her and the interpreter's daughters, the mother of the twins. But they never treated the family. The twins were willing to break with the tradition and help, but they were not licensed in Massachusetts yet.

The interpreter endured the shot silently.

He liked that his doctor prescribed a cream rather than shots. He imagined that the dream thieves would inhale it and suffocate. Or get stuck to it, and he would catch them in the morning and hand them over to the dream cops. Or they would escape, but leave his dreams behind.

He applied the cream before going to bed. It smelled like lavender. Very soothing.

That night, he was a child in his dream. His mom bought him a rocking horsey with a long mane, blonde like his doctor's hair. But before he embraced the horsey, a thick, hairy hand, with the name Vladimir Vladimirovich tattooed on it, grabbed the horse's neck and snatched it out.

"Try more cream next time," the interpreter's wife told him in the morning. "The young doctors have no experience and set the doses wrong. A small dollop, huh! The level of precision! Try 50 milliliters. And use two pillows instead of one."

Mark Budman

The next evening, the interpreter's wife smothered his forehead with the cream.

As soon as he fell asleep, he was embracing the horse again, and the hairy hand appeared one more time, but now the interpreter was ready. He bit the hand. He heard the loud yelp, and the hand was gone, leaving a pile of shiny bitcoins behind.

He woke up to a gentle neighing and saw the rocking horse on his side of the bed. It was smaller than he remembered, but even more handsome.

"I told you so," his wife said, touching the horse's mane. "Nothing beats experience."

When brushing his teeth, he found them covered with blood. And there was thick hair stuck between them.

The next night, after applying the cream, he slept well, but without any dreams. When he woke, his forehead was covered with the remnants of planes, ashes of planets, the cooled-off stars, and unborn fiction.

Tooth, Claw,
and a Few Bucks

Joe "Bud" Williams III owned most of the essentials of the typical rural New Yorker: a 12-gauge shotgun, cheaper-than-dirt Smith and Wesson semi-automatic compact pistol, a snowmobile, a non-working jukebox, orange hunting overalls, five pairs of size 42 jeans, five matching blue denim shirts, two plaid button-downs, ten baseball caps, six muscle shirts, and two pairs of boots (one for everyday wear and one for church).

When his third wife Betty (the first died, the second left with a truck driver) brought home an antique pillow from Russia, Bud didn't pay attention. Busy as a squirrel in an oak tree, she brought all kinds of stuff to their family nest. But when he learned that she spent $120 on it, he exploded.

"Do you know how long it takes me to make 120 bucks?" he yelled, shaking his sizable fists at her. Red blotches sprouted all over his face. He wore his favorite baseball cap, one size fits all, with yellow plastic mesh in the back, the words "General Hardware" on the front, and plastic sunglasses attached to the visor to shade his mud-colored eyes.

Betty retreated to a corner, both hands in front of her freckled face, low enough not to cover her eyes, which were the color of the winter sky. She had been married to Bud for six years, and she knew he wouldn't touch her, but she had to make a show on his behalf. Let him think he was the boss. She was more upset about the heatwave than about his usual yelling. Even after five straight days in a row of ninety-degree weather, Bud had refused to buy the cheapest one-room air conditioner.

"It ain't that hot Upstate," he'd said. "The heatwave only happens maybe a couple of days a year." Then he turned on a window fan to bring a steady stream of warm, muggy air.

Betty knew that Bud worked at an air-conditioned place but she had no idea how long it took him to make 120 bucks. Judging by his take-home pay, it took a long time, but she would be hard-pressed to be more exact. After all, he may have had some other outlets for secret spending. Men did things like that.

It took her twelve hours to make $120 at the burger joint.

Still, the pillow had been irresistible. It practically smelled of exotic lands filled with palm trees and pink flamingos, something she had never seen in real life but longed to explore.

"Don't, Bud," she said now, trying to sound pleading, and wiping the sweat from her brow. "I don't complain when you buy your teddy bears."

Bud stepped back and lowered his fists. "What's wrong with my teddy bears?"

"Nothing," Betty said soothingly. "I love them, too. Especially Cherished Teddies."

Bud grunted.

"I'll sell it! I promise!" The whiff of exoticism from the pillow had begun to disappear, replaced by the heavy odor of reality. Bud was right. 120 dollars could have been better spent. They needed a new fridge, and the kids kept outgrowing their clothing. They grew like weeds, God bless them.

"Promise?" Bud backed away some more. The red blotches began to fade from his cheeks.

He was glad for her excuse to back off. Unlike his friends, he had never hit his wife. His buddy Stu just got three to five for breaking his wife's nose. His other buddy, Mike, had been about to get a few years in the pokey, too, but he hit a tree while driving drunk on his snowmobile. Now, he chilled in hell. The olden days of male freedom were gone.

"Promise."

"That's my girl. Hey honey! Do you know that honey is the only food that never spoils?"

But Betty had no idea where to sell the pillow until a strange woman phoned her a week later, and said she would drive over to buy it. She sounded lady-like and foreign like Julie Christie from the *Doctor Zhivago* DVD she had bought at Wal-Mart for five bucks. She didn't like the title much, but the price was right. The Doctor turned out to be cool and educational. Betty didn't realize that Russians had their own civil war, trains, theme songs, and such passionate love. She even cried a little. She decided that she would watch the movie again sometime, and she refused Bud's request to sell the disc on eBay. Bud hated everything foreign. He voted for Trump and kept saying that the wall with Mexico had to extend to shield the coasts, too. And the skies. He read on Twitter that the illegals can fly over in hot air balloons.

"See this cop sitting in ambush behind the store?" Penelopa said after Piotr and she drove for over an hour through what Penelopa called the Redneck Country. "He's probably

Mark Budman

the village's main source of revenue. But don't worry. He's not a spider, nor are we insects. We are law-abiding citizens."

At twenty-nine miles per hour, Piotr caught the glimpse of the policeman's sunglasses, large like a predator's eyes, and shuddered. They were not citizens. They were not law-abiding. They were insignificant. They were flies. They were mosquitoes. They were butterflies. The cop could eat them alive, and then get a pat on the back from the mayor. They got out of the rental car in front of a clapboard house situated on a few acres of Otsego County, some of New York's least desirable real estate. Two rusty cars sat on concrete blocks in front of the house, next to an overturned super-market cart. Another car, probably in operation since it still had wheels, stood in the driveway; it bore a bumper sticker that said, "Keep honking, I'm reloading." A raven searched for under-the-wing fleas on a wooden rooster half a man's size. A shabby brown mutt came to greet the partners with a loud bark.

Piotr felt very uncomfortable without his familiar tall buildings around him, without the soothing presence of crowds, without the honking of the cars and the smell of ex-haust. Rustic air seared his urban lungs, and he had a nagging feeling that the too-big, too-bright sky with its country-style fried egg sun would fall and crush him to death in this wilder-ness.

A man in jeans, an orange muscle shirt that read "I'm the NRA and I vote," and suede boots came out and removed the mutt. His jaw was the shape and size of a brick and the same color—red-brown, with a few black dots. A cleft that might normally grace the face of a B-movie actor sat in the bottom part of the brick. Sparse yellow whiskers grew under the man's nose and on his hands.

People like that, Piotr thought, don't wash their hands after doing 'the deed' in the public toilet and therefore make the door handles dirty. Damn them for all eternity.

Once inside the house, the man pointed to a sofa oc-cupied by a small tabby kitten. The TV that sat inside a stand of laminated wood showed a football game.

There was a teddy bear on every horizontal surface. Some were traditional, soft, and furry bears—party bear, graduation bear, wedding bear, boy bear, girl bear, granny bear, and even military police bear with its dog tags. But the majority were teddy bear porcelain figurines—each a few inches tall. A teddy bear with a snowflake, a teddy bear next to a Christmas tree, a teddy bear surrounded by bunnies, a teddy bear in a hot air balloon, a teddy bear eating honey, a teddy bear inside a spaceship, a teddy bear trinket salesman, a Bar Mitzvah bear, and a teddy bear on a sleigh. The only missing version was a pearl-seeking Russian bear and its side-kick.

Bears, Piotr thought, the smile of a commissioned salesman glued to his lips at the wrong angle. Only foreigners think bears and vodka symbolize Russia, so this guy's clearly not of Russian descent. Not smart enough to belong to the intelligentsia, and not spiritual enough for a Russian *muzhik*, a peasant. On the other hand, he mused, America has a habit of draining brainpower from even the sturdiest intellectual, and spirituality from even the most thick-skinned *muzhik*. I guess if I'm lucky enough, Piotr thought but did not say, and they let me stay in this country, I'll have a bunch of beer and vodka bottles in *my* living room a few years from now, and I won't even notice the depth of my depravity.

Despite Bud's second invitation to the sofa, Piotr remained standing because the kitten hardly moved. He didn't like cats; their bodies were covered by bacteria-laden saliva, and they shed indiscriminately. Moreover, they were unreliable and not trustworthy. Just like humans. Even the best of humans, such as his partner, who had been on her way to becoming an almost sister to Piotr despite her constant scheming and unpredictability and a failed attempt at sex.

"Who's winning?" Penelopa said. She, too, didn't sit down. She wore a red baseball hat, its visor backward, its adjusto-strap displayed prominently across her forehead. The hat had no logo; she had explained to Piotr that a wrong logo would create more problems than it solved.

"Empathy, my friend, empathy," Penelopa had kept repeating while driving. "That's the key to successful negotiations. Let him think that you are his friend. Let him think you are his sister. Or brother, whatever. Better yet, let him think you are bringing him money."

"Buffalo Bills and New York Jets... You talk funny, lady," Bud said now. "Where are you from? Mexico? Canada? Europe?"

He pronounced "Europe" the way one of the prominent American leaders of the past did—"Urpe."

"No, we actually just came from Rio De Janeiro, Brazil. Like I told your wife, my name's Penelopa and this is Piotr. We love football. All we see in Brazil is soccer. Football is so much better than soccer. Soccer is for wimps."

Penelopa made a face as if she were chewing on an aspirin tablet, and Piotr was quick to follow. If Bud didn't get the signal that they both hated soccer more than anything else, he was obviously a space alien.

"You got that right, lady," Bud said. "Soccer sucks. It's cheap. All you need is a uniform and a pair of sneakers. What did you say your name was? Penny Lopa?"

"Yeah. You got that right."

"I'm Bud." He shook the duo's hands. His hand was as rough as the dirt road that led to his house and as muscular as the bull they had seen grazing in a nearby field. People with hands like that are good at bowling, Piotr thought. He had played once and had hated every minute of it. But had the man brought up the subject of bowling, he would be willing to praise the game. Ziggurat, what we do for your sake, he thought.

"What can I do you for, guys?" Bud said.

"Like I said on the phone, we are here to buy your pillow," Penelopa said. "We are not collectors. We are buying unwanted stuff. So people like you could have a better investment for their hardworking money."

Piotr nodded vigorously while wiping his hand on his trousers behind his back.

"Sure, the pillow," Bud said. "Betty!"

A thin woman wearing a flower-patterned dress came from the next room. A rusty-haired toddler in nothing but a diaper held onto her hand, his thumb in his mouth.

"Here it is," she said, handing the pillow to Penelopa. "I paid 150 bucks for it. We can't sell it for a penny less. Right, Bud?"

"We need to make a profit," Bud said. "We got kids, you know. Kids want to go to college."

"How about a trade?" Penelopa said, holding onto the pillow with both hands. "I can offer you a valuable limited-edition Chinese vase. It will make a nice addition to any house. You will be the envy of all of your house guests."

"Why would I want your rinky-dink vase?" Bud said.

Piotr glanced at Penelopa. He didn't know what "rinky-dink" meant and suspected that Penelopa didn't know either. But if Penelopa indeed didn't know the meaning of the word, she hadn't shown it.

"Because it's not rinky-dink," Penelopa said, bobbing her head. "It's a genuine treasure worthy of being displayed at any museum in Urpe."

"This vase is an object of beautification," Piotr said. "Polish, pulchritude, and refinement. I mean, polish in terms of eternal grace, but not in terms of being made in Poland."

Bud and Betty exchanged glances. The toddler waddled close to Piotr and tugged at his sleeve. Piotr gave him a dirty look but was too afraid to move.

"Bring it in," Bud said. "Let's check out your rinky-dink thingy."

Obeying Penelopa's gesture, Piotr went to the car to bring in the vase. His hands shook so much he almost dropped it. Then he imagined the fury that accident would have brought, and he shivered. He placed the vase on the table.

"It's a very unique antique vase," Penelopa said. "If you ever decide to sell it, any antique dealer will pay you at least three hundred dollars. I can give you a certificate of authenticity, free of charge. With such a certificate, the dealers will fight over it."

For a few long minutes, Bud examined the vase and the certificate Penelopa had printed the night before after downloading and doctoring a sample from a Web site of an antique store. She had been careful to print it on the best heavyweight, glossy paper.

"Pay attention to the exquisite flowery pattern," Penelopa said, pointing to machine-applied paint. "It's typical for the XI Ming Geo Banh Dynasty. Emperor Myao Dzun practically ate out of it. Just ask any art historian. Or Google it."

Bud grunted. The toddler sat on the floor and attempted to untie Piotr's shoelaces.

"I could offer you one more thing," Penelopa said, producing a sheet of paper. "This is a legal deed to one acre of the moon. The moon property is the hottest selling object in the world. It's suitable for framing."

Bud took the paper for closer examination. His lips moved while he was reading the text.

"Here's my card," Penelopa said. It used to belong to an antique dealer, but it belonged to Penelopa now, so technically that wasn't a lie.

"OK, Mr. John H. Greenback," Bud said and extended his hand toward Penelopa. "That vase, the deed, and fifty bucks. Cash."

"The vase, the deed, and twenty bucks," Penelopa said, clasping his hand. "Or my employer will fire me and my children will go to bed hungry."

"Bosses are a pain in the ass," Bud said and shook his head. "My boss is a piece of shit. They all are, you know."

"I'll tell you a joke," Penelopa said. "A boss comes home and sees his wife with one of his workers...."

"Where did you get the deed?" Piotr said when Penelopa and he were back in the car. He held the pillow with both hands. They had to part with thirty dollars and that hurt. Not for long, they hoped.

"From the same place as the certificate."

Noticing that he frowned, she added, "Relax, partner. When we sell the pearls, I'll buy you a real porcelain vase instead of this ceramic shit. I'll fill it with Swiss chocolate and French cognac. I'm generous. You've noticed it, haven't you?"

"I did," Piotr declared solemnly. "You're the most generous human being I've ever met. My heart trembles when I think about you."

"That's the spirit, boy. You'll have to pay half of the cost, naturally. There is no such thing as a free gift."

Naturally, Piotr thought. Nature is cruel. Red in tooth and claw, but green in the bucks. Not as cruel as people, though.

He closed his eyes and decided that if this pillow would be empty, he would kill himself.

He didn't.

Here Comes the Sun.
A Divus Story

When we are children, we are afraid of monsters invading our dreams. Eventually, it seems like the monsters stopped coming, but they are only dormant, sleeping in our memory cells. When we turn old, we will know they will return, and we will never wake up, unless we're lucky enough to die facing our loved ones, with our eyes open.

But the interpreter is not worried about that. He knows how to keep the monsters under control: he befriends them. He's practiced this technique since he was bullied in his childhood.

He fancies himself a reincarnation of his friend and adviser, the Biblical Joseph. He Photoshops his head over a coat of many colors and pastes himself a staff in his hand. In the next pic, his head is attached to the body of a viceroy of Egypt. He wears a *khat*, a cap crown, and a white kilt.

He shows the result to his grand-twins. They point to the image excitedly. That's pretty! Let me touch it! Me too!

He hopes that when they grow up, #MeToo will

mean: I've also gotten a raise. Or, I'm also promoted. Or, I'm also elected to Congress.

The interpreter is proud of his computer skills. He always learns something new. At the age of two, he discovered that girls' geometry is different from boys'. At the age of three, he learned the Cyrillic alphabet. At the age of five, he learned that a fist in the face is painful. At the age of six, he learned the English alphabet. At the age of sixteen, he learned that if you write poetry, girls would like you, and let you create new geometrical figures together. At the age of thirty, he learned that a new language is difficult to acquire when you're over ten and that freedom means different things to different people at different times.

He always tries new things.

At the age of twenty, following Winston Churchill, he tried to have a heart. At the age of thirty, still following him, he tried to have a head. At the age of thirty-five, he wrote his first poem in a language that wasn't his. At the age of forty, the neighbor's wife, a Mrs. Robinson, was after him at a block party, but he escaped, leaving her holding his beer.

He took his interpreter certification exam at the age of sixty. At that age, people usually administer exams rather than taking them. But he was proud.

He contemplates starting a Facebook page where he would interpret dreams.

Dreamed of climbing up inside a steel pipe? It means it'll be raining soon, so beware of falls. Fell off a tall, stone wall and broke your head, and no one could put you together again? You will have eggs for breakfast. Lost in the woods and heard the howling of a wolf? You will buy a Ralph Lauren cape. Easily satisfied with the very best? You read too many Churchill quotations.

This page would be much more popular than his current one, "Politics. Please be Civil." No one wants to be civil in

Mark Budman

politics. It's a painting in black and white, and it's all screams and rage.

Throughout his workday, he daydreams when he has a rare break. He sees an old man slouching in his office chair, with a headset on his head. He wears a shirt of a single color. The man's face is lined as if exposed for years to the Egyptian sun. The man speaks in two languages simultaneously, from both sides of his mouth. Words of wisdom and words of silliness. That's what having a heart and a head really means. To be wise but not be afraid of making fun of yourself. To defend your world against the pharaohs and Hitlers, but to be tolerant of the views of others. Joseph and Churchill knew that.

He hopes that the twins will learn it, too. That's why he's still here.

On the weekend, his wife and he are taking their well-deserved time off on the beach.

The interpreter rolls up his shorts high and wades into the shallow water up to his knees. In addition to shorts, he wears a t-shirt, a floppy hat, and a bandanna. Whatever may be exposed to the sun, is covered by sunscreen with SPF 50. He doesn't like the UV light too much. It causes pain when people get a sunburn, and even more so when they suffer the consequences years later.

Planes land and take off from the nearby Logan airport. They fly low and their bodies momentarily block the sun. Seagulls block it, too. Most of the UV gets through, though.

The sandy bottom of the lagoon is littered with broken shells. Weeds hug the interpreter's legs. The hair-wide fishes dart back and forth. A little crab fingers the interpreter's foot with its claws, checking if the man has started to rot yet. The interpreter pulls the crab out of the water, and it tries to hide within its shell. The tips of its bone-white claws are sticking out. They look like the fingernails of an old

Russian-speaking patient he was interpreting for on several occasions. She was getting worse and worse, and she died, screaming for the whole world to hear, during his morning shift. It all started with the sun exposure for her. People have too much skin.

She hated the sun, she said, and its rays. It's killing us, she said. Is it the face of heaven? Where are we to hide? Underwater?

Do you consider me a *divus*, a lesser level of divinity than a *deus*? the interpreter asks of the crab now. Someone who can make a conscious decision about your life and death? You probably think that a *deus* is too high for you, right?

The crab doesn't respond. Maybe out of fear. Maybe because it considers itself stoic. Maybe it thinks a mere crab is not worthy to talk even to the lower-rank *divus*?

Do you know that there is a similar word in Russian? *Divo*?

The crab is still silent. It doesn't have a head to nod.

But maybe the reason it doesn't reply is that it's sick and needs a medical interpreter to communicate with the provider? How does one interpret for a crustacean that is lucky enough not to have skin that can be damaged by the sun?

The interpreter lets it go. He returns to his towel on the sand. A seagull eats another crab a few yards away. The crab is still alive, wiggling its legs. The interpreter is sure it's not the same crab. This one is bigger, more mature, and more reserved. The seagull casts an evil eye at the interpreter, the eye of a *divus*, and then returns to pecking.

The interpreter lies down on his towel and dreams about a life in the parallel universe where he knows the language of everyone and everything without being a *divus*, and where the sun is less deadly, and no one is afraid to lift their faces to the heavens.

Mark Budman

No Country for Flying Men

Most people fly in their dreams, especially when they are young, but the interpreter never loses this ability with age. Moreover, he flies when awake. It's got to be some kind of disease because healthy and reasonable people don't fly in real life, but he does. It's not a communicable disease because his parents, his brother, and his childhood friends didn't catch it. Even his wife hasn't caught it during their thirty years together.

He can't rise too far anymore; he only flies indoors, and he only reaches the ceiling and no higher. He tried to fly outdoors many times, but since his childhood, he hadn't succeeded to rise even a centimeter, let alone an inch, in the open air.

Because he can't fly high, he reminds himself of an anchored woman from Chagall's *The Promenade*, but that's still more than an average ground-bound man can do.

The funniest thing about this is that no one pays

attention to his flying. People take it or pretend to take it, as normal. When he floats to the ceiling, they just raise their faces to him, and continue their conversations as if nothing out of the ordinary happened—or in the case of his wife, they keep berating him for having such a short memory, or for not getting the garbage out on time, which is one and the same.

He has tried to tell them about his abilities, of course, but they just nod politely or grunt impolitely. He's considered wearing a placard on his chest: *See, I am flying*. He used to believe in the power of the written word. When he was little and was able to fly up to the clouds and beyond, he read someplace that the human iris is black because there is nothingness behind it. And he contemplated sticking a needle in his eye, reasoning that it wouldn't hurt him because you can't hurt nothing. Now, he knows better: words can lie and therefore they do.

Even now, he floats near the ceiling in his 107-year-old friend's apartment, and even this friend says nothing about the interpreter's flying. This friend used to be a cavalryman in his country, in Europe, back in the 1930s, but now he only mounts a wheelchair and needs help even for that. They speak in a mixture of Russian and Romanian, with a smattering of English. The interpreter's native language is Russian, and, according to most Americans, he has to know Romanian by definition. Most Americans are convinced that Romania is "part of Russia," and the Romanian language (as well as Polish, Bulgarian, Czech, Slovakian, and Serb) is a dialect of Russian. That's innate knowledge, and you can't convince them otherwise, and that's why the interpreter learned the most important phrases in any language: "I love you," "Leave me alone," and "Is dinner ready?"

His wife also knows a few. "As you wish," "Can't you see I'm busy?" and "I'm so tired."

The interpreter's friend lives alone in an assisted living

Mark Budman

apartment. His children, kids the interpreter's age, come to visit, too, but their paths rarely intersect. The interpreter works in a medical office, interpreting for patients with limited English proficiency, so he's deeply knowledgeable about all kinds of diseases. But his knowledge doesn't end with medicine. His friend and he discuss health issues, politics, history, and science. The interpreter is an expert in all of these fields.

When he flew in front of his friend for the first time, the interpreter hoped that the old man was old and wise enough to comment on his flying, but he didn't. Maybe he couldn't see well?

Now, the interpreter tells him about his dream. That he stayed at a beach-front hotel hit by a giant tidal wave. He ran up the hill, but the water kept coming after him.

"Would you interpret it for me?" he asks. Usually, he interprets everyone else's dreams, but a practitioner can't treat himself.

The friend doesn't miss a beat. "You will meet the love of your life, and she will drown you in her attention."

After the visit, the interpreter goes to see his daughter. Her twins play on a carpet. He reads them an illustrated book about the adventures of a band of doggies in the movie theater while bobbing up and down next to the ceiling. It's their favorite book, and he has read it to them a dozen times. His wife sits on the floor, listening.

"Why *Deda* flying?" one of the twins asks. Neither of them ever asked this question before. He wonders if they didn't notice before, or didn't know how to ask. Or were just ignoring him like everyone else.

"Because *Deda* thinks high of himself," his wife says before he manages to answer.

"So, you also noticed me flying?" he asks his wife. "Why have you never mentioned it?"

"Because I was afraid you would fly away."

"Was afraid? But not anymore?"

"No, because if you fly away, I will follow you."

"But you can't fly."

His wife rises to the ceiling and bobs up and down next to him. The twins watch them with wide-opened eyes.

"When did you learn?" he asks her. "How?"

"I didn't learn it. Flying is a contagious disease."

She takes his hand, and they read the book together, bobbing up and down in perfect sync.

Mark Budman

Low Flying Children

The Green Man stands alone on the sidewalk of a new housing development where every house is at least half a million in Earth money. He wears a red cap and holds a matching red flag, and a sign, Slow. His eyes are undiluted anthracite with speckles of white. His skin is poison-green, the color that makes you think of an industrial spill. His main purpose in life is to warn the cars that there are low-flying children in the area.

The steps to accomplish that are down-to-earth simple: if the car goes fast, he has to slow it down. To do that he will:

Engage its brakes. If that doesn't work, go to step 2.

Push the driver's leg off the gas pedal. If that doesn't work, go to step 3.

Blow up its engine.

The Green Man doesn't stoop to anything physical. Just like the minister or wedding officiant says, "I now pronounce you man and wife," and the couple are. So is the Green Man. He thinks, "Now you slow down," and the car slows down. A leap of faith for the newlyweds. A leap of faith for the drivers. Unless they are both faithless and imaginative. Then they don't stop. Instead of taking it metaphorically, they go and find a real cliff to leap from.

The Green Man stands less than three feet tall and is slow by nature and design. They left him here months ago, and he hasn't moved an inch, hasn't changed his awkward forward-bending pose. At night, when it quiets down, the Green Man imagines himself coming from Mars. Not because he's aggressive and warlike, or because of the color of his skin, but because he's mysterious.

The Green Man's not very talkative. He talks neither to the tiny ants that crawl across his body nor to the butterflies that meet for a cup of tea on his cap. But there is a single creature, an earthling, he suspects, who talks to him. It's the old interpreter of dreams and illnesses, also known simply as a medical interpreter, who's pushing a double baby carriage with his two grandchildren every weekday. He's twice as tall as the Green Man and not quite as stooped. He knows many languages of this and other worlds. He stops to say hello in Martian. The Green Man doesn't reply, but he winks when no one is watching. If someone still sees him anyway, they'd think it's a design or manufacturing flaw. A malady of a kind that needs no interpretation.

The interpreter's grandchildren, who are out of the carriage now, find something on the ground, and shriek, "bee, bee!"

The interpreter bends over.

"It's not a bee," he says. "It's not even alive. It's just dirt. It has never bee-n alive. Let it bee."

He laughs at his own joke. The grandchildren pull out the blades of grass and weeds. They know he will protect

Mark Budman

them no matter what.

"Is there life on Mars?" the interpreter asks of the Green Man.

What kind of question is this? Of course, there is. The Green Man is so offended that he doesn't reply.

The interpreter persists. "Say, would you like to be young forever?"

The Green Man wants to say that he's already young and will stay so forever because plastics are virtually indestructible, but he bites his green tongue.

Before serving here, he worked at Miriam's house, far, far, far away (the number of "fars" was limited only by the observer's imagination).

Miriam, the woman of sugar, hated the rain. She was born on a rainy day, and the nurse at the hospital had a hard time pricking her heel for a blood test. At first, they thought Miriam had diabetes, and that clouded her mama's day, and her milk turned sour. Who would like rains after that?

Every time it rained, Miriam's mama put a long, ugly coat on her, and waterproof pants, too. Kids laughed at Miriam because of that. Worse yet, some water drops got on her face, and left deep, ugly spots on her cheeks. Mama had to cover them with a fresh coat of sugar powder, but that didn't happen until the end of the school day, and Miriam had to walk with a pockmarked face until then.

When she grew up, she married Michael, the chamomile tea guy. They were practically made for each other. They had four children, each sweet and calm, and the newly enlisted Green Man stood by their house, silently asking every vehicle to slow down, until one car didn't and almost hit all four of them.

And then Miriam and Michael took the Green Man and exiled him far away, to the Old Man's planet. They placed him in the steerage of a spaceship full of immigrants, refugees, prisoners, deposed dictators, failed magicians, and malfunctioned androids, to be deposited on primitive worlds.

Now, the neighborhood children, those little shrieking elves, flutter around the Green Man. They haven't knocked him down so far. The cars are few, and they all drive under the speed limit. The drivers have children, too.

The Green Man dreams that one day he will throw away the flag and depart for home in a bug-free rocket ship. But not before the children grow up, walk instead of fly, and drive cars of their own. He's sure the interpreter will see him off. Otherwise, no one will explain the Green Man's departure, and the former children will be sad.

Because he has so many gifts as compared to the Earthlings, he knows that before he departs, one day, Testudinidae, aka the newly hatched, wild baby turtle, will want to cross a vast expanse of asphalt from her birthplace to her next destination. She's a free spirit; she doesn't belong to anyone, especially to humans. They hide their skeletons on the inside. They must be ashamed of them.

Testudinidae will not know if this ground is a driveway, or a road, or a path to eternity, but she will not care. She'll want to get to the other side, and she'll have never chickened out in her life yet. Her tail is a masterpiece, which is a story in itself.

She'll watch an old man, who will be even older by now, pushing two toddler strollers at once. A big toddler in each will hold enough toy animals in her hands to fill up a baby Noah Ark.

Each stroller will have eight wheels. Testudinidae will guess that means there are sixteen altogether. A high chance that at least one of them will roll over her yet soft shell. Will she live to be sixteen? She'll think it'd be sweet if she does.

She will keep crawling. The wheels will be rolling. The toys will be falling. The old man will be singing to his grandkids, oblivious to the ground dwellers.

There will be two possible, mutually exclusive outcomes:

The Green Man will blow off the stroller's engine, and the world will survive.

The Green Man will not blow off the stroller's engine, and the world will become burned and empty.

The old man will stop to watch the suddenly glowing skies.

No Blood

The interpreter crosses the lobby of the second biggest hospital in Boston while attaching his badge to his lapel. He wears a gray jacket and navy pants, his favorite costume, and he hopes that no patient will puke or bleed on him today. He knows better than to get too close to them, but sometimes it's unavoidable because they are often hard of hearing, and often forget their hearing aids at home.

He's scheduled to work three hours today. He will make $51. He'll be rich. Another day like this, and he'll buy an Amazon Prime membership.

His size 13 triple wide shoes beat on the tiled floor. Pain pulses through his arthritic feet. He doesn't come here often anymore; he prefers to work from home. Sometimes he misses the human touch. But not the human vomit on his hands.

At home or with his friends, the interpreter dispenses free medical advice to everyone, whether or not they ask for

Mark Budman

it. Exercise daily. Don't skip breakfast. Stay away from processed foods and red meat. Get off your computer or smartphone an hour before going to bed. Or, if you don't, at least install a blue light filter for your screen.

He talks about politics, too. He says, "Trendy people kiss the ass of a prevailing wind." He came up with this meme on his own, and is immensely proud of it.

Here, at the hospital, he just interprets what the patients and the medical providers say. He's not allowed to express his political opinions or dispense advice while working but has to make sure that all parties understand each other.

It doesn't mean the interpreter is not learning new things here, too. He picks up multiple pearls of wisdom. For example, cutting your veins in a bathtub full of filtered water and antibacterial soap is the cleanest death. He's ready to add this to his repertoire of free advice.

He arrives at the office. It's a cognitive impairment test. The provider, a middle-aged man, asks an old woman, a Russian speaker, all the standard questions in English. And the interpreter, naturally, interprets back and forth.

"Memorize three words. Apple, penny and table. You will need to recall them later. OK?"

The woman nods.

"Repeat after me," the provider says, "Apple, penny, table."

"Apple, penny, table."

"Good. What year is it now?"

The patient thinks hard. "1818? No, 1918. I have no idea."

Last night, one of the twins said, "One idea can't be bundled together."

The other one replied: "It's a good idea."

The interpreter agreed. It's a good idea not to be empathic in medicine. An interpreter has to repel human misery like a goose repelling water. Otherwise, he'd be sick himself soon. But repelling doesn't always work.

Now, the provider takes notes. The interpreter also takes notes, lest he introduces his own errors into the test. He shuffles his feet. The woman dozes off.

Two nights ago, one of the twins wrote her first flash fiction story. "My hair soft. Pretty. Me happy."

The interpreter posted it on Facebook. He got three likes and one passionate rebuke for posting copyrighted material without an express release from the author. Afterward, he read "Aeronautic Engineering for Babies" to the twins. He flapped his hands to explain how the birds fly. They followed his lead and rose three-quarters of the way to the ceiling. Just for a very short time, unfortunately.

"Can you recall the three words?" the provider says now.

The woman straightens up. "My father was a cavalryman back in 1892. He had a bay horse. Brown body. Black mane and tail. Her name was Vanda."

The provider takes notes. The woman dozes off. To calm himself, the interpreter thinks about a buzzing dental drill.

He rarely interprets for dentists. They do not get federal money, so they are not required to have interpreters. The patients would have a hard time talking with their mouths full of dental tools anyway.

His dentist told him when the interpreter sat in her chair with his mouth open, "I like you. You're funny."

All women, including the medical providers and the patients, like him now. It's no danger to confess your love to a harmless grandfather. One patient once asked for his phone number.

"You have such nice, mature eyes," she had said. "Reminds me of my husband when he was your age."

Mark Budman

Now, by the end of the test, he is ready to bite both the patient and the doctor. But he remembers the dental implants that made a more than $10,000 hole in his budget, and he restrains himself.

He says goodbye to the patient and the provider. He fills out the form for his payment. He waits for the elevator.

The other day he shopped at CVS. He asked a young lady with a nose ring for directions to the foot care aisle. She looked at him, her eyes slightly unfocused. "We don't sell fruits."

"That's comforting to know," the interpreter said, "but I'm looking for foot care."

"Food is aisle 9."

"Not food, but foot care. There is no such a thing as 'fruit care aisle' or 'food care aisle' anyway. What would it even mean? But you do have a foot care aisle."

Her eyes focused on him. "You have such a terrible accent," she said. "Spell it."

The interpreter sighed. "S-e-n-s-i-t-i-v-i-t-y," he said and did what he should have done in the first place: looked for the foot care aisle himself. His feet hurt.

When he limps out of the elevator, in the lobby, he sees a woman lying on the floor. Blood is flowing slowly from her nose. A few people surround her. No one is saying anything.

The interpreter sighs. It's not his business. This is a hospital. Tons of providers. The chances she speaks Russian are remote.

He raises his ID like a badge of honor.

"Let me through," he shouts. "You," he turns to one of the onlookers, a young guy with a goatee. "Call 911."

He takes another step. There will be blood.

Yet Another Study of Woman

Her full name was Precious Rose Jewel, courtesy of her mom, who had been committed to a mental institution at the age of twenty-seven when Precious was eight. Her mom claimed to be the daughter of Elvis Presley and a "famous poetess" whose name she had never revealed but said was "A-Number 1" in the literary world and beyond. Through the poetess, Precious's mom traced her origins to Honore de Balzac. She had collected rag dolls, buying them in huge numbers from antique stores, and Precious had a vague memory of her mother in a flaming red dress, her eyes glowing through her unkempt hair, sprawled on the pile of soft, limp bodies with a book in hand; that's how Precious's love affair with collectibles had started.

During the evening meal, her mother would tell the same story. She worked as a secretary at a "large firm" and her boss "took advantage of her" and then "laid her off." Until much later, Precious didn't know what "taking advantage" meant, but she imagined that the boss asked her mother to hand wash his underwear—that's what Precious's father kept asking of mom, and she hated that. What "laid off" meant, Precious hadn't even begun to comprehend, and that bothered her almost as much as Jake Lee's pestering her at school.

Unlike her mom, Precious collected all kinds of things, from thimbles and porcelain figurines to limited edition Norman Rockwell ceramic plates, which she bought for investment purposes. She even had a signed and numbered print by Dali, her most treasured possession. She wasn't sure if she could make sense of the tangled-up images on the print's surface, but as long as the future buyer could, she was fine. Her three curio cabinets were overflowing, and the mantel on her fireplace had no room for even a speck of dust.

When she met John, she appreciated his love for collectibles. So what they were military knives? She married him.

Five years later, while visiting New York City on a day bus trip arranged by her employer, she bought a Russian antique pillow from a private home. She was still excited about her audacity. To go to the apartment of an unknown person (it was a woman, but nevertheless) was out of Precious' character.

She was strolling in Greenwich Village when she saw an ad with a photograph on a community bulletin board. The pillow was pitch-black, with flaming-red needlepoint depicting the Russian Imperial two-headed eagle. The vivid contrast of the two colors struck Precious' fancy like a baseball bat. Moreover, it was just like the pillow her Russian-born grandmother Vera had owned. She called it the *podushka*, a Russian word for the pillow, which literally means "under the ear." Precious remembered playing with the *podushka* when she was a little girl, hugging it, pressing it against each ear at the time, and eventually spilling milk over it. Grandmother spanked her then, and Precious refused to talk to her for a week no matter how many cookies the poor woman had offered her. She ate the cookies, though, and then stuck out her tongue at Grandmother. She was a bad girl, bad.

Now, Precious called, and a woman answered. She had a kind voice, and she happened to live within walking distance. The risk was high, but the temptation was irresistible.

A woman in a black evening dress and with earrings the size of bagels with everything opened the door for her. She led Precious through a seating room into another one that looked like a small-time antique store. Precious had had to maneuver her way around chairs, statues, curio cabinets full of bric-a-brac, mounds of stuffed animals, sewing machines, and the like. The air smelled of mold and dust.

"I'm practically selling it at cost," the woman said when they finally sat down. "$150."

The pillow lay on a small stool between them. Precious had a hard time keeping her free hand off its velvety surface.

"I don't have much cash. I can only offer you $100. Will you take a credit card?"

Woman or no woman, Precious still held her other hand in her purse, on the button of her cell phone that would automatically dial 911. Prudence was her motto and way of life.

"I can't process that." The woman stared into Precious' eyes. "You know what? Since you're a visitor to our city, I'll sell it to you for $120 in cash and a $10 check. We, New Yorkers, have to be nice to visitors, you know. We want you to keep coming back to our beautiful, friendly city. You have a checkbook with you, don't you?"

Precious read naked greed on the face of the seller, and her fingers gripped the cell phone tighter. Her other hand stroked the pillow again. What if it held a treasure from the old world, like in that Mel Brook's movie, what was its name?

Mark Budman

She understood that she had no choice. This woman had seized her collector's heart and wouldn't let go.

"$100 in cash and a $20 check," she said. "A penny more, and my husband's gonna kill me."

Even $120 was too much. A printed circuit designer's salary didn't leave much room for fancy. Especially now, when the boss in the corner office spent all his days behind a closed door, which probably meant an impending layoff. And John's preacher's income wasn't enough to sustain even a small family like theirs, the two of them and their two girls.

Ah, a layoff. She knew what it was now, and knew all too well. That was the thought she tried to suppress. It was like Damian's sword hanging above her. Or was that David's? She didn't remember which hero gave his name to the saying. Bosses were so cruel, having only their interests in mind. Of course, they pretended to serve the stockholders. Duh! They served only their egos and pocketbooks. She watched on TV how gangsters kidnapped rich people in Brazil for ransom. Would the same thing happen in this country, too, when the bosses would transfer all jobs abroad and everyone but them would be poor? And what for? Just to make $150 million a year instead of $100 million? Why would a human being fall that low? That was a puzzle to her, and she resolved to crack it one day.

If you believed John's fiery sermons, the bosses would be burning in Hell for all eternity. As far as she was concerned, that was a bit too much. All eternity was a pretty long time. If it was up to Precious, she would limit their burning to perhaps ten to twenty years, with a possibility of parole for good behavior. And she would force them to be low-level office workers for the rest of their sentences.

Sometimes she had second thoughts about that. Take the way they treated the layoff, for example. Not telling any facts, not giving any warnings, and letting the rumors grow like weeds in the garden. In the company cafeteria, she and her coworkers watched the bosses for telltale clues, but the future Hell inhabitants kept poker faces. At that point, Precious was ready to damn them for the whole of eternity.

And yes, she slept with the new pillow under her ear now.

Today was the day Precious had dreaded for the last several months. One could never be sure, but the rumors had flown in a dense formation, like mosquitoes after the mowing of a lawn. The night before, she had dreamed about the people of her department assembled in a conference room. The head manager told them that the staff remaining after the layoff should be proud because they were "survivors." All clapped, but not Precious. Not that she didn't want to, but her hands were tied behind her back.

The head manager, a petite woman of uncertain age whom they called Alice the Hun, turned her evil eye on Precious, and said, "If you don't clap, your name will be included in the next layoff list."

Now, Precious regarded the blinking light of her work phone as if it were the eye of a cobra. Her office mate Linda's phone wasn't blinking. Precious turned to Linda, and the other woman returned to her keyboard quickly. Precious said a quick prayer John had taught her, picked up the receiver, dialed the password, and retrieved the message. It was the last person on earth she wanted to get a message from today— her boss. "See me at your earliest convenience."

He would usually tell her ahead of time what this conversation was about. This time the subject was absent. That wasn't good. It wasn't good at all.

She walked down the aisle like a zombie, turned right at the coffee machine, and smashed into a woman carrying a drink. Two men, plastic cups in their hands, watched the collision, their mouths agape. The woman gasped. I look terrible, Precious thought.

Some of the coffee landed on her white blouse; she didn't feel anything. She mouthed an excuse and continued her trek.

The boss motioned her to close the door to his office. His office was identical to hers, except he shared it with no one.

"Precious, you know that our company is in terrible financial shape. The orders are not coming. We can't justify so many people. We are in the midst of restructuring now. You have been selected to be laid off."

Selected to be laid off, she thought. It sounds like I'm winning a prize. His lips were moving, which probably meant that he was continuing to talk. His precise words no longer registered in Precious' consciousness, but she was sure he wasn't taking the previous statement back.

Precious stared at him, a rubber smile on her lips. She had never been laid off before, so the whole process was alien to her.

"Why me?" she finally managed. "Am I a bad worker?"

"It has nothing to do with your performance," the boss said. His head was shaped like a pear; two fresh nicks showed on his pencil neck. His graying black hair was parted in the middle. Rumor had it he wore an earring outside of work; Precious had never seen him outside. For all she knew, he lived in his office, leaving it only for meetings, lunch, and bathroom trips. Maybe his wife was sending him fresh shirts daily and visited him on annual family days for sex and pro-creation.

"We have the formula to rank everyone," he continued. "Your rank is lower than others."

Precious thought about what to say for a moment. A haze covered her line of vision. She had to go on talking, though. That much she knew.

"How much lower?" she managed to ask.

What am I saying, she thought. Is that important? Am I going insane?

"I'm not at liberty to discuss that," the boss said. "But here's a package to help you prepare for the transition. It answers all your questions. We offer a lot of benefits, more than an average company of our size. We will even give you $500 for any educational courses that might launch a new career for you."

He pushed a tall stack of papers toward her. Her name was handwritten on the top of the first page in the boss' neat cursive.

"I have to take your badge," he continued.

Precious couldn't judge his emotions. Was he happy to let her go, to exercise his powers over her? Or was he a sympathetic human being? She decided he was happy. She wouldn't be happy if she were him.

She unfastened the cloth badge holder she had about her neck. The holder was dark blue, with the word "idea" printed several times along its length. They gave it to her when she came up with an idea of saving printer toner, $125 savings a month according to the company's financial wizards. They gave her a $10 gift certificate for Barnes and Noble as well. She had spent it on coffee. Before she had received the holder, she used to clip the badge to the collar of her blouse or her sleeve, wrinkling them or even losing the badge once in a while. The badge was a small rectangular piece of plastic with her photograph (she looked stupid and ugly on it), name, and serial number as if she were an inmate. Its bottom was beginning to delaminate, and she had failed to open the entrance door a few times already because she couldn't insert the badge in its reader.

She was about to get a new one; too late now. She

handed the thing to her boss and watched him clip it to his collar. He wore his badge on a holder similar to hers, but he had the name of the company printed on it.

"If you have any questions, don't hesitate to ask."

She had too many questions to formulate any of them. By the time she came to her office, the haze had cleared somewhat but it was too late to go back and ask. Even if it wasn't— and she didn't know for sure since she had never been laid off—she wouldn't be able to force herself to face the boss again anyway. She saw a silent question on Linda's face and shrugged.

"Like it was expected," she said. "I'm out of here."

They hugged and Linda cried. Precious wanted to cry, too, but not a tear came out. Constipation of tears; the stupid thought kept circulating along the paths of her brain.

"I'm ashamed," Precious finally mumbled. "Maybe I did something wrong? Maybe I'm a bad person?"

"You did nothing wrong," Linda said. "They worry about the stockholders. Yeah, right. They only worry about their pocketbooks."

Linda helped Precious arrange her possessions in a discarded copy-paper box— a family photograph, a porcelain figurine of a clown, several old copies of *National Geographic*, a poster of a cruise ship, an inspirational plaque John had presented her when they got engaged, and, of course, her beloved Russian pillow. Oh, the pillow! Just touching it would give her joy. A heavy cloud of mystery surrounded it, though John had denied the existence of any non-sanctioned mystery, of course.

Linda helped her load the box into Precious' car and then they embraced.

"No more lunches in the cafeteria," Linda said, her eyes wet. "No more healthy walks around the block."

"I will miss you guys so much!" Precious said.

She didn't add that she would miss her paycheck at least equally as much.

"Us, too."

"You know my number," Precious whispered, fighting back tears. She lost; she felt a trickle down her cheek. "Keep in touch."

"Me next," Linda said and reapplied her lipstick. "I can feel it in my bones."

Precious didn't think so. Linda turned out designs faster than everyone else in the department. But one never knew in a situation like theirs; it was too unpredictable. It was like stock market fluctuations or hurricane patterns—beyond ordinary human comprehension.

On the way home, driving along a wet, deserted country road, Precious tried to sort out her emotions. Shame was really the most powerful one she had right now. She was surprised at herself. She thought she should be afraid of running out of money or about finding another job, but shame? Was she getting too sentimental for her own good? Perhaps she was getting old? Perhaps she was a bad girl? And then, that puzzle about the bosses. What motivated them? They couldn't spend their money anyway. Nobody could spend millions of dollars on one family; that was humanly impossible. So, what was the point of ruining everyone and everything? Were they simply mad like her mom, but in their own way?

At home, she Googled it, as she should have done a long time ago. It was "Damocles' sword," not David's. But Damocles may have escaped the sword, and she hadn't.

Then she checked the CareerBuilder for jobs. The sheer number of opportunities frightened her. Most were out of town, though. She sighed and clicked on the "Trending Searches" button.

A creative, motivated salesperson for door-to-door marketing of cemetery plots, no morbid attitudes, extensive

Mark Budman

travel required, will train... A Russian language interpreter for the National Defensive Shield Advisory Office, no recent trips to the Middle East or New York City, clean driving license, knowledge of Polish and Flemish a plus... A piccolo player for the Grand Bend, Pennsylvania Philharmonic, five years experience or more; will double up as security guard... An executive assistant—Master's degree or higher, proficient in Java and American Sign Language; should be able to lift 50 pounds and work in a smoking environment... A phone actress with a sexy voice for the ChatWithThePussy website has to join the union, tons of bonuses, money for Christmas... The Art Department seeks a wide range of applicants for three-hour modeling (nude) sessions in the classroom/studio; Permanent Resident or US Citizen, no jewelry in the pudendum area...

Another few days later, at the company's organized seminar, "How to find a better job and keep it," Precious got up and, following the lead of the workshop coordinator, said, "Hi, I'm Precious Walker. I have been laid off from Design Industrial Concepts after eleven years of hard work."

The audience clapped. Some were her laid-off co-workers, many of them the victims of the layoff that had happened six months before. Some were total strangers, probably victims of the corporate greed of other companies. Precious felt as if she were auditioning for an Alcoholic Anonymous reality show, similar to what she saw on TV. She didn't realize that so many people had been laid off this time because management kept it all hush-hush. The people here seemed like the cream of the crop of her company, so it was clear to her that management didn't know what they were doing, as always.

The coordinator, a young, cross-eyed woman in white slacks, sensible pumps, and a sleeveless blouse the color of dried blood mixed with ca-ca, beamed at her and said, "You are doing just great, Precious. A good first step. But remember to say that your job position has been eliminated rather than you were laid off. Don't sound bitter."

Precious tried hard not to sound bitter, harder than anything she had done for a long time. Her tightly compressed spring eased up a bit, and she giggled in the voice of her mom. When the coordinator asked the group to list the potential employers in the area, Precious was first to shout "Reliable Garbage," the name of her town's only trash removing company. When the coordinator asked a tricky question, "how do you address the recruiter if you don't know her or his name? Should we write To Whom It May Concern? Sir or Madam? What do you think?" Precious was first to cry, "Call him the heartless S.O.B!" When the coordinator asked them to compile a list of whom they knew, to be used for networking and references, Precious shouted, "I know my boss! He's a jerk!"

When the coordinator said that they had to improve their personal appearances to enhance their chances of being hired, Precious volunteered aloud that she would get the nose job she had always dreamed about.

"Well, that's not exactly what I meant," the coordinator said. "I meant shaving off a beard for a man, or perhaps dying your hair or having a more up-to-date hairstyle for a woman. But I like your creative thinking."

Precious wanted to say that she would shave off her hair to look more contemporary but bit her tongue. She remembered one of the marketing lessons she had been taught: when you are ahead of the game, slow down. And she was clearly ahead of the game in the coordinator's eyes.

By the end of the seminar, the coordinator had bestowed so much praise on her that Precious began to wonder if her boss would call her and tell her that he had made a big mistake by laying her off. Er, by eliminating her job position.

On the other hand, it seemed that she had rubbed off

some of her despair onto the coordinator who didn't sound so positive toward the end. Unless she was simply tired; Precious would be tired too if she were her. She could never understand people in the business of repairing the human psyche. Too unpredictable.

The closer Precious got home, the more she was convinced that the boss had called. So when she found no voice mail, she sat on the floor and wailed. Now she knew that she was a bad person and had to be punished. John would frown at suicide, an ultimate punishment, so she decided to cut her pillow to shreds with a knife.

She took her husband's Becker Necker, Carbon San Mai knife, admired its balanced weight in her hand, and thrust it in the pillow without hesitation. The material resisted, but she persevered with the determination of a Grim Reaper. After making at least a dozen cuts, she threw the knife on the floor, inserted both hands into the sad remains, and tried to pull them apart. The fabric was too tough. But when she turned it upside down, a small wooden box fell out. When she opened it, she found a shiny stone inside. A faux pearl. It had to be faux. It was so huge. She played with it for a while. It was too big for a ring. Maybe a pendant? Then she saw a folded sheet of paper with something scribbled in Russian. It took her 15 minutes to decipher the text. It said: "Not this pillow."

She stowed the box away in her drawer, threw out the remains of the pillow in the garbage, ate a chocolate bar, and cried.

When a woman with a Russian accent called her the next day with an offer to buy the pillow for her aunt, dying back home in Russia, she instantly recognized a fellow sufferer and agreed to sell the pillow for whatever price the woman offered.

A Dancing Giraffe

The interpreter of dreams and afflictions is past his prime. He has been this way for ages, and it stopped bothering him years before. His dreams bother him, though. His official title is a medical interpreter. He even has a badge to prove it.

Interpreting can be a dangerous occupation, even if they pay you in dollars. Ask the people who used to help the Americans in Afghanistan. The medical interpreter's work is not nearly as dangerous, but it can be unpleasant. He has to navigate carefully between the parties who can't understand each other, and sometimes don't want to.

The interpreter doesn't say it aloud, but trying to placate some people is like pissing a mixture of ethanol, gasoline, and cooking oil on glowing embers. He keeps it to himself for two reasons. Firstly, if he says it in English, he would have to interpret it in Russian. That's a lot of work. Secondly, if he says it in any language, he would be summarily fired. He's not ready for that yet.

Mark Budman

He's interpreting for a patient, an old lady who wants disposable bed pads and adult diapers free from the insurance company. The patient is officially called an LEP, which stands for Limited English Proficiency. That means the patient knows how to say, "I want" and "you have to give me" and "I know my rights" in badly accented English. For the rest of the conversation, the LEP speaks in Russian, and the interpreter has to do what he's hired for: to interpret the conversation between the agent and patient. The agent is also an immigrant, so all three speak in a language, not of their own.

The interpreter is interpreting remotely, sitting in his home office. It's beyond magic: the providers touch the screen in their office, and the interpreter is summoned like a genie from a bottle, in all his glory, image, and sound, but no thunderbolts and no smell of sulfur. This time around, the interpreter doesn't even see the patient and the agent since the interpreting session is audio only, so he can stand and make a face at them or flip them the finger.

"My friends told me I can get silk panties and lined chiffon robes as well," the patient adds in Russian when the pad business is completed. "You can't deny me. You don't want me to walk naked, do you?"

The interpreter has no choice but to interpret that. The insurance agent pauses.

"Are you translating this correctly, translator?" he asks, making a too common mistake of calling the interpreter a translator. Earlier, a doctor called him an interrupter instead of an interpreter. A Freudian slip.

All news is calling the Afghan interpreters translators. It's like claiming that the soldiers and the Afghans were exchanging written documents in the heat of battle.

Interpreting is the facilitation of spoken or signed language between people of different languages, cultures, education, ages, and health. Some may be sick, tired, angry, rushing. It could be noisy. People have accents. They are not professional news anchors—they may not pronounce words accurately. The interpreter has no time to think, to check the sources. The translator deals only with calm, measured texts. The translator has it easy.

The interpreter wants to say that he has to interpret accurately no matter what nonsense he hears, but he's afraid for his job, and he pisses gasoline on the embers: "yes, sir," and the agent explodes like a flashbang grenade. Except the bang hits only the interpreter.

"Are you getting fresh with me, interpreter?"

"No, sir. The interpreter is just answering your question, sir."

"Don't you 'sir' me. I will report you to your management."

Two hours later, the interpreter reads his two-and-a-half-year-old twin granddaughters a book about a socially and physically awkward giraffe. Eventually, the giraffe overcomes his inhibitions and learns how to dance in public. On the last page, he dances with a whole band of animals in a forest clearing.

"Where are the animals' diapers?" one of the twins asks.

The interpreter tries hard but fails to find a sufficiently witty and educational answer. Actually, he has three.

The animals are short on cash.

The jungle stores ran out of diapers.

The animals here are adults.

The problem is, none of the answers are any good, neither witty nor educational, and the last one is not even true. Some adults need diapers and use disposable bed pads, even if they dream about silk panties and lined chiffon robes.

A bit later, one of the twins points at the new issue of *Time* magazine, with a naked baby on the cover. "Where is the

Mark Budman

baby's shirt?"

"Her insurance denied it," the interpreter says. "By the way, I must tell you, the beginning of life is like the end of it, at least intellectually."

When the kids are asleep, the interpreter reads a book about a woman who wanted to go to exotic countries in Asia, because she's bored with her rural Middle American life. The interpreter has been to exotic places himself: Moldova, Ukraine, Moscow, Volga River, Siberia, Mari Republic, Kazakhstan. It's rural America that is exotic to him.

He wants to go to North Dakota or West Virginia and rent a room in one of those houses he's only seen on TV. He would sleep in a canopy bed or on a straw mattress or on whatever thing the natives usually sleep on. He would listen to crickets and owls and chickens and wolves and coyotes and bison before falling asleep. He would hope to hear a wolverine, the most exotic creature he's read about, which would be tough since he has no idea what it sounds like.

In the morning, he would come down to have breakfast with the house owner, whose name is Bud or Duke or even Chester. He's an old country gentleman-beatnik, long-haired and bearded, in faded jeans and flannel shirt, chewing tobacco, while simultaneously smoking weed and drinking rye, and the interpreter would ask him a troubling question:

"If you were a superhero, what superpower would you want to have? As for me, I'd like to be able to regenerate like Wolverine. Be forever young, imagine that? No need for the claws."

And Bud or Duke or even Chester would mumble something so profound that the crickets would chirp the Ode to Joy, wolves would do synchronized howling, the wolverines and even some stray giraffes would dance, the chickens lay platinum eggs, the earth would shake, and naked, diaper-less owls and crickets would fall from the skies on little gold parachutes.

And there will be no need to interpret that or to placate anyone or explode in rage. And the ethanol would be only used to make stiff drinks, gasoline to propel the vehicles, cooking oil to cook, and the fire would give out only warmth. Even a socially awkward giraffe should understand that.

Mark Budman

The Invisible Man

On the night before his flight to Israel, the Interpreter of dreams and afflictions watched the Ukrainian national anthem sung in Yiddish, and *Katyusha* in Chinese, on YouTube. His Facebook handle was "Interrrnationalist." With three Rs. Two hours later, he had one of his usual nightmares. He ran through a brick-walled labyrinth. A flight attendant was close on his heels with a Turkish *kinjal*. She ran fast despite her high heels.

In the morning, the Interpreter posted an elaborate reflection on his dream on Facebook. He received eight likes, with various emojis, but one female friend called him a misogynistic Zionist and a creep. Before he was able to reply that some people are dying to be perpetually outraged and that he feels sorry for them, she unfriended and blocked him.

Two days later, the Interpreter walks alone on the gravel path toward the shrine in Bahá'í gardens in Haifa, up the side of Mount Carmel. It's easier for him to keep his balance on gravel than on the asphalt. It's so hot here. He almost sweats, though he's thin. He wears a sensible floppy hat, cotton pants, and a cotton short-sleeved shirt. His sneakers are size 14. Tourists like him are few.

A gaggle of Arab kids on a school trip runs in the opposite direction. He can't tell the difference between them and the Jewish kids. He knows they can.

On the last workday before the trip, the Interpreter was interpreting (what else?) for an old patient, even older than himself. At work, he was a medical interpreter, with a small "I."

"You speak Russian so beautifully," the patient said, smiling at him through the doctor's office iPad. "Are you based in Moscow? I'm a Muscovite myself, but I live in Chicago now."

The Interpreter worked from his home office in Boston, via his camera-equipped computer, but he wasn't supposed to discuss that, so he only smiled.

"I'll be discharged from the hospital soon," she said. "To my home in heaven."

The Interpreter dutifully repeated her words in English. He wasn't supposed to add anything personal. He was supposed to be transparent. Be either a machine, a part of the office equipment, or an invisible and featureless cyborg, with politeness and the need to take bathroom breaks being the only human features. He was supposed to use personal pronouns for both the doctor and patient. Like this:

Doctor: "When was the last time you menstruated?"

The Interpreter: "The last time I menstruated was thirty years ago."

Doctor: "Did you have any abortions?"

The Interpreter: "I had two."

Mark Budman

Now, in Haifa, the Interpreter stumbles. He drops his sunglasses case. Before he bends through his arthritis, a girl picks up the case, turns toward the Interpreter, and hands it to him. The Interpreter remembers that the tour guide told him to talk to people only in English or Hebrew. The Interpreter rushes through his meager ration of Arabic words. "*Shuhran*," he says. Only then did he remember the Hebrew word for thank you. "*Toda*." Too many languages to memorize.

On the last workday, the doctor told the old woman that he had to give her a physical exam.

"I have to give you a physical exam," the Interpreter said dutifully, in Russian.

The old woman stumbled. Then she laughed. "How will you do that? You're inside the box."

The Interpreter wanted to say that he's always outside the box. But that would pierce his invisibility cloak. So he just soldiered on. He wished he could post this encounter on Facebook, but he was afraid it would breach the woman's confidentiality.

In the morning, he wrote it down, in English. English was his language of nightmares. Yet the flight, on the Turkish airline, was uneventful. Security even screened the flight attendants for sharp objects.

Now, in Haifa, he snaps pictures with his digital SLR. The green living arches, the white concrete vases, the gold-and-black wrought-iron gates. He can post *that* on Facebook.

Bahá'í faith keeps its garden open to all regardless of religion, or anything else. Just like America, cough, cough, cough. Just like Facebook. Except that Facebook can be vicious. Unless you want to remain invisible, which he cannot.

The Interpreter keeps walking up the hill. They say

the heavens are closer in Israel. If he keeps walking, he will get there before his appointed time. The Facebook people wouldn't notice. They'd think he blocked them. People often misinterpret other people and get outraged and combative easily. It's hard to disarm them, but he can try kindness.

Mark Budman

Tick Tack.
You are Dead

The Interpreter's wife points to a tiny black spot on the white wall of the foyer and screams, "It's a tick."

The Interpreter is schooled well. He's a professional conduit for those who don't understand another language and an amateur conduit for same-language speakers who don't understand each other. He's also a grandfather of twins, and everyone knows that the twins demand strict discipline.

He takes a pair of tweezers he uses to extract tiny fish bones that stick between his teeth and catches the creature. He deposits it in a clear plastic bag. He needs to take a picture, upload it to the web to make sure it is really a tick, and not, say, a ladybug. He's working with medical professionals, but he's not an entomologist so he relies on others on this subject.

The Interpreter comes back with his SLR camera, but the tick suspect is too small. And it crawls around too fast.

Should he buy a macro lens? It would take a day to mail order it. He doesn't believe in going to a brick-and-mortar store. But the unfed tick would die in 24 hours, or so he's learned from Google.

"Is it ethical to starve a deer tick to death?" he asks aloud. "It's cuter than a fawn. Not to me so much, I admit, but to his mom. Ticks have moms, right?"

"Kill them all," his wife says. "They spread Lyme disease."

She's normally not bloodthirsty. No, she's never bloodthirsty. He's trying to interpret her words, fails, and settles for a joke. "Would the jury of its peers approve?"

"It's either us or them."

He thinks he's seen that meme on Twitter.

The Interpreter pricks his finger and drops a tiny droplet of blood into the bag. Though he's a humanist, he's not a speciesest.

The tick dies anyway.

The Interpreter goes to the backyard. It smells of wild strawberries and deer droppings. Squirrels squawk. He's an intruder here.

The Interpreter buries the tick in a shallow grave. He doesn't know if the tick had any name, rank and serial number, but he makes a tombstone for him from a stick, and attaches a piece of paper that says "Here Lies Tack. He Crawled Too Far."

In the morning, the Interpreter finds that someone, probably a deer, stepped on the grave and overturned the tombstone. Nature is red in hoof and horn. He interprets that from the humanistic point of view: from subjective experience Tack no longer cares.

The Interpreter returns to the house and takes out a carton of buttermilk. A bold red warning is printed on the carton: "Lyme Disease Kills. May contain milk."

Mark Budman

He pours some salt-free, sugar-free cereal. It may contain wheat and it may contain no sugar or salt. Time for breakfast.

His wife screams from the foyer, "It's a tick."

The Interpreter gets up and walks to the foyer, muttering to himself, "Being a Humanist means trying to behave decently without expectation of rewards or punishment after you are dead."

Kurt Vonnegut said that. He knew how to interpret the language of nature. He was also a writer, like the interpreter himself. An even better writer, truth be told, but not as proficient in medical interpreting or the art of digital photography.

The interpreter wonders what would have happened if Vonnegut would be able to put his hands on the eternal youth serum. Would he learn digital photography, too, or would he spend the rest of his youth just writing?

Either of those two options would beat death. Tack would agree.

Lex Talionis

The car crawls on a twisty country road between two cemeteries. The one on the left is older, and its tombstones are thinner by far. Perhaps the people of yore were less corpulent or flashy. The newer cemetery on the right is flush against the Wall. Its dead would suffer first if it breaks. And the dead do suffer, no matter what the living might tell you.

There is a lake downhill, so the dead on both sides have a nice view of the fishing boats, and the runoffs from the cemeteries feed the fish. You have to pay for the view. Poetic justice. The law of retaliation. Lex Talionis. Eye for an eye.

Personally, the driver, the grandfather, *deda* in Russian, likes tooth for a tooth better. After all, some people have thirty-two of those versus only two eyes.

One of the three-year-old twins in the back seat says, "I don't like these statues."

"They are tombstones," the grandfather says in English. His wife wants to talk to the kids in Russian, but she's

Mark Budman

not here now.

Among the three people in the car, he is the explainer-in-chief. He sits in the front because he's also the designated driver.

"What are tombstones?"

"The stones that mark the place where the dead people lie."

"What is dead?"

"Someone who can't walk or eat ice cream or build castles from blocks or read to a child or write fiction. It happens to old and sick people."

The other twin says, "Why aren't you dead, *deda*? You're old."

"Because I have to drive you. If you have responsibilities, you're not allowed to be sick or die."

"When we learn how to drive, will you die?"

Deda is contemplating this. According to the mirror, he is still young and handsome. But that might be a fairy tale he is too anxious to believe in.

A few minutes ago, they had to stop to wait for the Wall crew that blocked the road. The Wall always needs repairs, lest the desert gets in. Or the flood. Whatever is currently happening behind the Wall.

No one wants that. They all know what the desert or flood would do to the people, animals, trees, and plants. Even the twins know.

A cop was regulating the traffic.

"What is his name?" one of the twins asked, pointing to the cop. *Deda* had to name every man and beast, and some inanimate objects, too.

"Well, since he is enforcing the law, his name must be Lex," *deda* replied.

"And that guy?"

"Since they work together, he must be Talionis. You

see, if Mr. Talionis falls and hurts his eye or breaks his tooth, what would happen?"

"I don't know," the twins said in unison.

"There is a common misconception that Mr. Lex would have to knock out a tooth or hurt the eye of his Environmental Protection Agency supervisor. But it's not true. The Agency just has to pay for the damages. That's the true meaning of *lex talionis*. Anything else is just falsification or ignorance."

That was easy. The question about death was harder. When we learn to drive, *deda*, they asked, will you die? In other words, once you stop being useful, should you just fall away? Like this Wall would if everything suddenly goes back to normal like it was before the Catastrophe?

"I hope I'll find something else to do for you, besides driving your own grandkids around like I'm driving you," *deda* finally says.

I'm inventive, *deda* thinks. I'll teach them how to catch a fish rather than buying them a fish. More importantly, where to get the rod and the line and the hooks, and how to find a place where the fish roam. And how to make sure no one would take this fish away. That's how you survive in the world.

Or I'll come up with something even better. Like something that would let them not just live forever, but use their lives to improve the world and help humanity, whatever is left of it.

If *deda* repeats this thought several times, he'll have no choice but to believe it.

There is some natural justice in this.

Mark Budman

A Reflection on the Fountain of Youth

The certified interpreter of dreams and afflictions buried Lyubov in the middle of May. Her name meant "love" in Russian, and she was as lovable as her name suggested, if aloof. She never complained, she never hurt anyone, and her very presence soothed even the angriest souls.

After the burial, the interpreter, the wannabe most excellent immigrant of his generation, stood with his head bowed. A white and pink snow of fallen petals covered the backyard of his overpriced condo. The petals formed intricate layers, spelling out messages of sorrow and consolation in all the world's languages.

Delivering the eulogy as Lyubov's friend and legal guardian, the interpreter declared that she died of a broken heart, in her sleep, and that she was golden through and through, up to and including her heart. If anyone deserves eternal youth, he said, it was her. Not eternal life, mind you, because who wants to be senile and arthritic forever? But eternal youth, health, and vigor.

The guardian buried her under an old oak tree that shed acorns and rotten branches on the roof of his 10-year-old Subaru. He jury-rigged a tombstone out of a thank-you card and wrote an epitaph: "She ate worms. Now, they eat her." In truth, Lyubov ate fish food, but he allowed himself poetic license. Most epitaph writers do.

There were no attendants at the funeral except for a curious chipmunk that oozed charm by the spoonfuls, a chattering squirrel with the world's bushiest tail, and a neighboring cat gazing through his window. The interpreter knew the cat; he was a Turkish Angora, his claws were the size of *yatagans* and his eyes were the color of the raging sea.

Lyubov had everything an imprisoned fish could possibly desire: a comfortable and spacious aquarium, plentiful fresh water, food, pumped air, and solitude. Did she die happy or in pain? She didn't tell.

In a Russian fairy tale, an old fisherman caught another goldfish, just like Lyubov, and she offered him three wishes in return for her freedom. Perhaps Lyubov, too, had offered, but her fisherman took the wishes and broke his word. Or perhaps she was born in captivity and never knew freedom. Or, maybe, the last wish of the fisherman was that Lyubov should spend the rest of her life in the aquarium of an old immigrant, and die there.

Or, maybe, she was not a goldfish at all, since gold is heavy, and yet when she died, she floated to the surface.

After giving Lyubov an honorable funeral, the interpreter was driving to his daughter's house, repeating silently the opening of his newly minted bestseller "How to Heal the World in Seven Easy Steps."

"The world is sick. Medically, politically, economically, and spiritually. Someone needs to heal it. I can do that. I have the powers and the drive. No one asked me, but I volunteered.

My first advice: don't look for the day everyone has the same opinion because then humanity will cease to exist."

Actually, he'd minted only the first chapter. Even that wasn't complete. He had written the first seven sentences, and even though they existed only in his head so far, but they were brilliant, promising, and uplifting. The next step was to write them down, upload them to the cloud and then bring them down to earth for execution.

He was driving to his daughter's house, while his otherworldly mentor Joseph, the viceroy of Egypt, the standard of male beauty in the Bible, and the owner of the coat of many colors, rode shotgun. Joseph didn't wear his seat belt, but no cop could see him, of course.

Even if the cop saw them, the fear of Joseph would've fallen upon him, and the cop would have let them go with just a warning, and watched them drive away with an expression of awe on his face.

Neither the interpreter nor Joseph said a word. They talked only while the interpreter was dreaming, and though the latter loved multitasking, he found sleeping while driving dangerous.

In his youth, the interpreter had been as handsome as Joseph, at least according to the interpreter's wife and to a few young ladies before her, who by now had become middle-aged-to-old ladies, if they'd survived the rigors and afflictions of their Soviet, post-Soviet and even immigrant lives.

The interpreter didn't tell anyone about Joseph, even his wife, his best friend and most caring critic, lest he is accused of harboring imaginary friends at his age, or worse.

As if Joseph's presence during the day is not enough, the interpreter dreams about him one night out of seven. This night Joseph is dressed in scrubs and a stethoscope, instead of his coat of many colors and *keffiyeh*, or instead of his later uniform of a tunic, pleated petticoat, and striped headcloth.

"You will find the secret of eternal youth from one of your patients," Joseph says, neither in Biblical Hebrew, nor in ancient Egyptian, but modern Russian. "Use it wisely."

Joseph is not the interpreter's childhood hero. They didn't know each other until the interpreter turned middle-aged. Joseph is his hero of old age.

"If a patient tells me something, I won't be able to use it," the interpreter says. "Not even on Twitter. HIPAA rules. What's the point of knowing a secret if you can't use it?"

Joseph checks his watch in a doctor-ish manner: discreetly, but not overly discreetly. "You'll be able to use this secret, but only for yourself."

The interpreter wants to say that HIPAA would still be mad at him, but he wakes up. His wife's space is empty and cold. She's an early riser.

Six nights out of seven, the interpreter dreams about his boyhood in a distant land, even more distant than the land of Joseph. He's seven, tall for his age, with curly black hair. He climbs up an ancient oak tree, and then onto the roof of a shed on his parents' property. He lies supine, watching the clouds move westward. His white cat Banditik climbs up, too, and settles on his chest. His loud purrs reach the train station five blocks away, and the trains smile.

The house used to belong to a single family, but now both it and the yard are divided in two. Hence, their yard is long and narrow. The future interpreter is somehow convinced that on the other side, behind a low fence, a treasure is buried. Books on magic, wizard wands and invisibility cloaks. All he needs is to get a shovel, climb over the fence and dig. And the treasure would burst forth like water from a fountain. But in his dream, he can never find this shovel. It's the neighbor's fault. The old woman who kept staring at him from under her white eyebrows must be a witch. Banditik always hisses when he sees her.

When he wakes up, the interpreter goes to the bathroom and rinses his teeth with warm salty water. Then he puts a hot compress on his eyes. He gets half of his medical knowledge through his wife, and the other half through being the online interpreter of afflictions.

His wife is a medical doctor. So were her parents. So is her sister. So are the interpreter's and his wife's daughter. The interpreter is the only one in the family with only a Master's degree, in Electrical Engineering. His wife has clearly stated that he is not smart enough to be a doctor. She is right, of course.

The interpreter shaves because of the demands of his job. He hates shaving. It's a tedious job and a waste of time. He cuts bits of himself and throws them into the garbage. How logical is that? How ethical? How environmentally friendly?

The interpreter is thin and tall. When he writes poetry, he describes his own eyes as piercing. He knows a bit about the fountain of eternal youth, Ponce De Leon, and telomerase activity. And Tithonus, too. He gets half of his knowledge about this subject from Google, and the other half from his subscription to *The Week*. One day, he will write a poem about Tithonus. It will be sad and moving. Evocative, as the critics will put it.

The interpreter plays with the twins while his wife is having a breakfast of hot water mixed with sugar-free cereal.

He shows off his new slippers to the twins. "My new slippers," he says in Russian and then in English. He enunciates the words clearly. He has the voice of a news anchor, though with an accent.

"No, no," the twins shout. "No new."

"I'm telling you they are new. At least they sold them as new at Walmart. Do you want to see the receipt?"

The twins don't look convinced, though they are

happy to tear the receipt apart. They were severely premature and spent over a month in the NICU, the neonatal intensive care unit, attached to various scary-looking tubes. But they are okay now, thanks to their grandmother's care. She's strict with them, in a good way: no TV, no smartphones, and no computers. Just educational games and puzzles and books. And a Doctor Kit, Pretend Play with Carrying Case. They are ready for Harvard medical school.

After a breakfast of fat-free Greek yogurt, salt-free cereal, and an overly ripe banana, the interpreter goes upstairs to his home office. He gets into his Staples special, the Executive Office Chair with Headrest-Breathable Leather, High Back, Black, sale price: $126.95. He turns on his notebook and the desktop computer. The former belongs to the company he works for and the latter is his. He adjusts his camera and puts on his headset. The wall behind him is covered with blue paper. He has two lamps illuminating him from both sides of the table. His patients and the medical providers will see him from the chest up. He wears a dress shirt, tie, pajama bottoms, and the new slippers, the world's softest, good for arthritic feet.

He spends a few minutes on Twitter and Facebook. Most of the posts are so severely lacking nuance that they could be as well painted in black and white. His posts, about his twins and poetry, are in vibrant color, of course.

He logs in to his work laptop.

When he has spare time between calls, which doesn't happen often, he chats with other interpreters on the company's chat board.

"Lost Worcester Memorial. *Каждый раз.*"

"Bad audio at Johnson City Regional. Не *слышно ни фига.*"

"Quick family emergency. Have to log out. *Бегу.*"

"Culver City rehab. Provider looked at me and hung

up. Я плохо накрашенна, *что ли?*"

"The patient was screaming that the doctor wants to poison him. *Какой идиот.*"

"Ladies and gents, I'm done with my shift. Have a wonderful morning. *Пойду спать.*"

"I confused the hell out of a social worker by telling her that the patient is Azeri. What the hell is Azeri, she asked. Is it a Russian dialect? *Дура набитая.*"

The interpreter suspects he's older than his colleagues. When he arrived in this country what seems like a hundred years ago, one of his friends was celebrating his fortieth birthday. The man was so old, ancient even, ready to fall apart at the slightest breeze. Now, the Interpreter's own oldest daughter—not the doctor, but the other one, the lawyer—has turned forty. What does that make him?

The interpreter used to go to the hospitals and interpret in person. He took the light train, the T. The other passengers were mostly young, but no one surrendered their seats to the elderly. They just sat there, faces buried in their phones, waiting to grow old.

At one point, the interpreter even had a Harvard email address because the hospital he worked for was in the Harvard network. He dutifully bragged about it on Facebook and Twitter. At that time, he knew for certain he was the oldest among his colleagues.

The interpreter's laptop buzzes now. The first session of the day commences. He pushes all other thoughts away. He's in total control. He's the only man on Earth who when told not to think about a white bear, succeeded in not thinking about it for more than a minute.

He sees the nurse's face on his screen. She looks bored stiff. Since his status is below that of a janitor, she doesn't hide her feelings.

He rattles off his introduction, in English. "Hi, I am

Alex, your Russian interpreter. My ID number is 12345XYZ. Everything that will be said here will remain confidential." Then he introduces himself to the patient. The same words, but in Russian. No one listens to the introduction anyway because it's just legalese. All the medical provider needs are his name and ID, but that is automatically displayed on the screen in the provider's office.

According to US law, every patient with limited English proficiency gets free interpreting services. Even if a patient is a millionaire from Russia. The service is free to the patient, but the medical providers have to pay the interpreting agency.

The first patient of the day is an old man, even older than the interpreter. Most of his patients are. The young learn English fast and don't need interpreters.

The patient sits in his hospital bed, chewing on something and chatting on a flip phone.

The English speaker is a young woman, a social worker. She looks stylish, in the interpreter's eyes.

"Sir," she says to the patient. It seems like she can't pronounce his name, Mr. Berezinsky. "Sir, I'm here to deliver you a letter from Medicare. Please sign that you received it."

The interpreter interprets everything dutifully.

Mr. Berezinsky stops chewing, closes his phone, and replies in Russian, "I'm not going to pay for this hospital stay. I can't afford it."

"This letter does not influence your payment. Just sign that you received it."

Mr. Berezinsky wiggles his finger at the social worker and then at the interpreter. "I love America. I love President Trump. But I was told that Medicare will pay for my hospital stay."

"This letter does not influence your payment. Just sign that you received it."

Mark Budman

"Do you know that my SSI payments are only $696 a month? I can't pay your fucking bills."

The interpreter thinks for a second and interprets "fucking" as "damn." He has some leeway in terminology, and the social worker is already blushing.

They go back-and-forth like that for ten minutes. Luckily, the connection breaks at this point. The interpreter reports dutifully about the lost connection on the company's chat board. He imagines the mismatched pair going on like that at least till the end of the workday, or maybe until Mr. Berezinsky's discharge from the hospital.

Last night, the interpreter took an online course about euthanasia and physician-assisted suicide, and the role of the interpreter in that. They'd counted over 2000 medical assistance deaths in Canada in 2017. They didn't have the US data yet.

"How well do you know yourself and your triggers?" the presenter asked. The word "trigger" is in fashion, the interpreter thought. Words are like flotsam or bricks. Some float and some sink. And then they take turns floating and sinking.

The interpreter must take courses like that for Continuing Education Units to maintain his interpretation certificate. He misses being able to drink. Drinking eases pain. Especially someone else's pain.

The interpreter's agency pays him $27 an hour. He used to make much more when he was an engineer before he lost that job. He holds twelve US patents, is fluent in two languages, has published some poetry, and considers himself a polymath. No one else does. Though he clearly states "polymath" in his Twitter profile. He has twelve followers. Half of them are bots.

The next patient is a young pregnant woman, beautiful as a model from a Botticelli painting ready for a C-section, but she wants a female interpreter. No one can blame her. The interpreter initiates a transfer. While they wait for the transfer, they discuss the three S's: Sutures, Stitches, and Staples. Which one leaves a less visible scar? The doctor is pushing what she calls a permanent suture while the model wants a biodegradable one.

When the interpreter's daughter was in medical school, she told him that when the students were learning about a new disease, they diagnosed it in everyone, including themselves. The interpreter felt the same way when he started to work in the medical field, but this went away quickly. Medicine wasn't a place for empaths.

He doesn't feel like he needs to have a C-section now.

The next patient is an old, obese man, who complains about his dry mouth. But it's dry only at night. The doctor is puzzled. The interpreter is dying to say that the patient probably snores and sleeps with his mouth open. But he's not allowed to interfere in medical decisions. The doctor orders a battery of tests. The interpreter will probably never know the truth. Continuity of care doesn't apply to him.

The new patient, bed-bound and frail, is also older than the interpreter. A nurse just removed her catheter, without even turning the camera away. The interpreter observed all the graphic details. A privacy violation on the nurse's part.

When the nurse leaves, promising that the doctor will arrive in a minute, the Interpreter sighs. A hospital minute can stretch for a long time. Not for eternity, but still longer than the normal measure.

Sometimes, the interpreter entertains patients while waiting. Sometimes he sings to them. Sometimes he discusses politics or the weather. Sometimes he reads his own poetry. This time he reads his poem, "Florida Antiques." It has been published in an e-zine with the word "review" in its name, which means that the e-zine is classy.

Florida Antiques

Here, the estate is a euphemism for death.
Dusty shades of silence
subdue even the brightest stones
and polished gold, and freshly touched-up cheeks

of a Roaring Twenties painted beauty.
Damn humid. Twisted shadows
palpate the nape of another woman's neck,
a living one.

A spider
contemplates the softness of her fingers
on a mahogany table where the matriarch dined
among a shrinking family circle.

The woman considers a purchase
to dine with her own family.

The patient listens. Not everyone does. Most people would interrupt after the first few lines.

"You look like my late husband," the patient says, in Russian, of course, when he's done. She's staring at him from under her white eyebrows.

The interpreter smiles as if he is flattered. He had mastered this smile some time ago.

"Do you want to be forever young?" the woman says. "I can tell you how to do it."

The Interpreter takes a sip of his herbal tea. He's used to complaints, shouts, threats, offers of marriage, and invitations to drop dead, but this offer is a first. Was she the one Joseph was talking about?

Last night, before taking his online course, the Interpreter taught the twins the difference between Phillips and flat-head screwdrivers. Now they can tell "fibis" from "fat." He also explained to them why they should eat wild rather than farm-raised fish. Because it has less mercury. And because "wild" is the opposite of "tame."

He could say that his grandkids are his eternal youth. Plato would agree. Unless it was Maimonides. Or someone on Twitter.

"How does it work?" he asks the woman now.

"That shouldn't concern you. Just say yes or no."

"Do you offer this to every interpreter?"

"Only to the ones who need it."

The Interpreter finds modern youth disgusting. They are overweight, rude, immoral, intolerant, lazy, and popular on Twitter. Who wants to be like that forever? Yet he's tempted to say yes, just to see how she would react. What if she gives him workable advice? Would he be tempted enough to try it?

"Did you try it on yourself?" he says.

"It doesn't work on some people.... So, is it yes or no?"

He adjusts his glasses. "Go ahead," he says. He can make a choice. He's not Buridan's ass. He's not anyone's ass. He's proud of himself.

"Is it a yes?"

"Yes, it is."

She recites a list of ingredients. "Mix them up and drink at precisely midnight in front of a mirror."

He records the list faithfully. Thirteen items. Most of the ingredients are available in the grocery store and a few in the neighborhood drugstore. The most difficult is a half-cup of fountain water. No crushed pearls, 22-carat gold flakes, or nightingale tongues fried in tiger fat. No unobtanium. He feels like he is watching someone else's dream. Not a nightmare, but a confused dream of someone who'd spaced out.

When his shift is over, he goes on a shopping spree and buys all thirteen items. At home, he locks himself in a bathroom and mixes it all with a silver spoon he was born with, according to his mother. He's done at quarter to midnight. He's staring at the tall glass full of chunky, greenish liquid. It looks like something healthy but disgusting. Just like a healthy drink should look.

He takes a sip precisely at midnight. It tastes as bad as it looks. He watches himself in the mirror, but nothing changes. His hair doesn't turn black, and his wrinkles don't disappear. He expected this. He's just wasted his time, and a bit of money.

He takes off his glasses. Strangely, he can see his reflection well, the same old man as usual, even without them. Even more strangely, he's hungry. He usually doesn't eat after 6 PM.

He knows there is nothing good in the refrigerator. Nothing good in the fridge. Just some stupid fat-free Greek yogurt and low-cal Halo ice cream. He needs to buy real food. Chips and pizza and beer would be a good start. Maybe he needs to go out. He hasn't done that for years. And where those stupid dreams are coming from? Joseph, huh?

"Greek yogurt my ass," he says. He's pissed at the old, sick broad who lied to him and at himself for believing her. He's not looking forward to taking care of the two brats downstairs. He needs a strong drink. He needs the sugar high. He turns away from the mirror, but the reflection of an old man, his face weathered by the sun, is still watching his back, dark, wise, and eternal.

The Interpreter's Wife

The interpreter's wife, the grandmother of the world's cutest and smartest twins, is aware of the passage of time, but she knows it's an illusion and a logical fallacy. The time doesn't go anywhere. Only we do.

She hasn't written a poem since before medical school. She was busy all her life, but now, after she retired, she has become busier than ever, taking care of the twins. Her husband isn't much help; as a matter of fact, he needs to be taken care of himself.

When they yet dated, he managed to convince her that he was handsome, smart, and reliable. As a future doctor, she realized that the illusion of time erodes even the most pronounced handsomeness, but being young, she fell for all three qualities anyway. That he was a poet, as well as an engineer and an inventor, and funny, was a small bonus.

In time, she realized that she was right about handsomeness, that his smartness was lopsided, and his reliability

Mark Budman

greatly exaggerated. As for funny, his jokes began grating on her nerves.

Like this one, though it might be not a joke but a true story:

A Russian-speaking psychiatric patient her husband was interpreting for found a kindred soul in him and would have been crying on his shoulder if not for her restraints.

Or he would call a patient who has blood clots in her legs Clotilda. Not to her face, the wife hopes.

Or he would tell this:

Doctor: Do you have memory problems?

Patient: I don't remember.

He claims these jokes help him to cope. His biggest joke is when he calls himself the interpreter of dreams and afflictions. He couldn't even interpret that the smell in the room comes from a baby who just pooped in the diaper.

When the wife worked, she never made jokes at the patient's expense.

When they travel with the grandkids, they take at least two bears, two dolls, one puppy, one kitty, and a plastic frying pan. That's besides food, drinks, wipes, and baby potties. Everything but the kitchen sink, the wife says. The interpreter listens. Next time, he brings a plastic sink. He thinks it's funny.

Now, the interpreter's wife sits surrounded by her granddaughters and him, and they reenact Russian folk tales: *Mashenka and the Bear*, *The Three Bears*—the Russian version of the *Goldilocks*, and the *Pussy Cat's House*. The interpreter plays either all the bears or the Pussy Cat's servant, the tomcat Vasya. To that end, he wears either a blanket and a fur hat, or a white apron and a broom. His mustache comes in handy in any case.

The re-enactment is in Russian, of course. The whole purpose is to teach the kids Russian. Russian is the lingua franca of the post-Soviet world, but being Slavic, it's technically neither lingua nor franca. But it's beautiful and helpful beyond the borders. It also stimulates the young brains.

The three-year-olds repeat their roles diligently, in funny American accents.

"Mashenka," the wife corrects them, emphasizing the first A and the softness of the N. "Mashen'ka. Isn't she beautiful?"

"The emphasis is on the first syllable," the interpreter says in English and then immediately interprets it into Russian.

"There is no point in saying it in English," the wife says. "They will learn it in English anyway. I know it's your job to interpret, but you're not working now."

He opens his mouth as if to say something nasty, but instead, he roars and flails his hands with pretend claws. The kids shriek.

"You scare them," the wife says. "They will have nightmares instead of dreams."

"No, they are shrieking with delight."

She knows he's wrong, that he just caters to their most primitive instincts, but she has no strength to argue.

Late at night, she's awake. This side of the earth sleeps soundly, and some sleep too soundly, having his dreams of healing afflictions. If she were a lesser wife, she would have confronted him and said, "carry your weight or else." If she were a lesser person, she would make fun of him because that's what gets through his armor. But she's better than that. She sees him through. Beauty is skin deep but so is male ego and bravado.

Last summer, he picked up a stone and chased away a barking dog when the grandkids cowed in their double carriage. When their second daughter was born, and she was busy with her medical residency, he babysat the baby, and she called him "mama." When she was pregnant with their first child, he spent all his free time standing in the infamous Soviet food lines.

Now, he drives them around for appointments, he's making a bit of money, he buys groceries, and the kids have fun with him, and worse comes to worst, there is someone for her to cry on his shoulder. Even the strongest woman needs that sometimes.

More importantly, she loves him and will never harm him. They say love is blind, but it's a lie invented by romance authors. Love has a hundred bright, sleepless eyes like Argus. Love knows and sees everything. So instead of a confrontation, she writes a poem:

Lot's Wife

To question is a crime
And to refuse is blasphemy.
If you take these rules with a grain of salt,
You will see your home
Destroyed by brimstone and fire,
And no one will remember your name.

She instantly feels better. Or shall she say, even better? Everyone knows that poetry is a powerful medication, without side effects and any burden on the health care system. But no one knows that better than a doctor. Especially if she's a woman.

Pillow 2.4

Several weeks after the interpreter found the pearls in a pillow, the doorbell rang at his Boston condo. There was an older man and a younger woman on the threshold. The woman, who clearly was the leader of the two, extended her hand and said *dobry den'*, which, as every medical interpreter who works with Russian patients knows, meant "good day" in Russian.

She projected pure assertiveness, a 100% lioness, the leader of the pride, while the man looked like a rank-and-file lemming, half-hiding behind his superior.

"Good day," the leader of the pride said, extending her hand and smiling from ear to ear. "My name is Penelopa. And this is my friend Piotr."

The interpreter shook her hand reluctantly. He stayed away from Russian speakers except for his wife and patients. He wasn't about to admit that he was an immigrant as well. That would lead to too many questions.

"I'm sorry to barge in so uninvited," Penelopa said. "We understand perfectly well that you recently bought an antique pillow of unknown origins. You see, it used to belong to Piotr's honorable late mother. It's dear to my friend's heart. The pillow is the only thing remaining that connects their once inseparable souls in the chain of eternity."

Like gas released from a tank, she seemed to fill all available space.

The interpreter stepped back. He trusted no men and only one woman. His wife. This woman looked reliably dangerous. She might have had a gun and or knife, but she surely didn't need it to take the interpreter apart.

"Please don't be alarmed," Penelopa said. Incredibly, her smile grew even wider. Piotr retained a Brezhnev-like scowl.

The interpreter was alarmed, and Penelopa's invitation to the contrary didn't fall on fertile ground.

"I think you should leave," he said in English, assuming his best American accent. He was hiding the pearls in a different place every day, and each new place seemed less secure than the previous one. Now he knew they were real.

"Name your price," Penelopa said.

"Hold on," the interpreter replied. He rushed inside the house and came back with the pillow. He had sewed it back carefully. To his eyes, it looked as if no one had ever opened it.

"$49.99 plus tax," he said. "The same I paid for it. I love it, but since it's your friend's only connection to his late mother..."

He knew he gambled. Probably the safest course of action was to deny having the pillow. First, he hated lying. Not only on moral grounds but because it could lead to unexpected consequences. Moreover, they certainly knew he bought it. It was stupid of him to brag about it on Facebook and Twitter. By telling the truth, he maybe could get them off his back. At least temporarily while he would decide what to do next.

Penelopa took out two twenties and a tenner. "Keep the change."

When they left, the interpreter washed his hands. After much thought, he took out a hundred-year-old can of pepper spray from the back of the pantry and moved the pearls to the bank safe deposit box. Then he spent a few minutes practicing his aim with the pepper spray, using a portrait of Stalin as a target.

Penelopa and Piotr showed up the following day. The interpreter met them with the pepper spray in hand. He was shedding stickers the twins had affixed to his shirt.

"Don't worry, sir," Penelopa said, grinning, in English this time. She was holding a folded sheet of paper in her right hand. "We come in peace."

Her accented "peace" sounded like a "piece." Piotr was nodding solemnly.

"And I want you to leave in one piece."

"Listen," Penelopa said. "We know you took the pearls. That's fair. I'd have done the same. But we have an irresistible proposition for you."

"Not interested."

Penelopa switched back to Russian again. "Let me just tell you what it is, in ten seconds or less. Elevator pitch. You don't need to answer right away. Please?"

The interpreter lowered his pepper spray.

"Yours was the last of the seven pillows Piotr and I were hunting for. All the other ones were empty, so you must have the right pillow. The pearls you found inside this pillow are more valuable than you think. They are the main ingredients of the youth serum that brings eternal youth. Now you have the ingredients but don't know how to use them. If you share only one pearl with us, we can make the serum and share it with you. Now we'll go and never come back. Unless you call us."

She placed the folded sheet of paper on the ground and left, followed by Piotr. The interpreter picked up the paper and read the phone number aloud. Area code 718. Brooklyn, New York. The nest of Russian-American life. Of course.

That night Joseph came to the interpreter in a dream. "Just do it," he said.

The interpreter was so tired that he didn't even get up from his bed to greet his mentor. "Why do you quote Nike's trademark?"

Joseph adjusted his *keffiyeh*. "I don't know what 'Nike' is. "Just do it" is a direct translation from ancient Egyptian. It means 'put your doubts aside and follow your heart.'"

"But I already tried so many different potions. None of them worked."

"Try this one and that's it."

With that, he left, and the interpreter had the next dream, about a patient who complained that Medicaid allowed only one free box of rubber gloves a month.

The interpreter suspected Penelopa and Piotr played him for a fool and wanted to pocket at least one of the pearls, but he went along anyway. Firstly, he still had another six. And what would he do with them anyway? Sell them? Make his wife or one of his daughters a necklace? Make a necklace for the twins? But which one? You can't make a necklace just out of seven pearls, however large. The girls would fight for it and instead of joy, it would bring tears. And he believed, perhaps mistakenly, that cooperation trumps confrontation.

Now he had a chance to advance the science of eternal youth. Even if he didn't quite want it or even if it didn't work for him, it was worth it to try. Joseph seemed to agree. Even more importantly, so did the interpreter's wife.

In the morning, the interpreter knew what to do. He called Penelopa.

"I will bring you one pearl. You'll get one chance."

"That's all we need," she said.

He refused to let them inside his condo, let alone his daughter's house, so they did the deed in Penelopa's and Piotr's hotel room.

"Multiple people know where I am," the interpreter told them. "Including the cops. No foul play. And I'm armed."

He was armed. With the pepper spray and determination to finish the quest for eternal youth once and for all.

The process of making the serum was kind of anticlimactic. Nothing electrical or electronic. No blinking lights or soulful music. No incantations. No rising fog. No goat blood.

Penelopa, dressed in a white lab coat and safety glasses, crushed the pearl with a gray granite pestle in a gray granite mortar and mixed it with some syrupy liquid. "We call it 'Ponce de Leon's Baby Breath,'" she said.

"This name has already been taken," the interpreter said. "It's copyrighted."

"We can use it because we are not selling the product," Penelopa said.

The interpreter was about to say that the copyright lawyers would probably object, but the serum was ready.

Each took a spoonful. It tasted like honey and cinnamon with bits of chalk for good measure.

Then they finished, the interpreter used his phone's camera to check his own face, but it looked the same. He didn't feel any younger either. Piotr also remained visibly old while Penelopa remained relatively young.

"Give it some time," Penelopa said. If she was disappointed, she didn't show it.

The interpreter gave it an hour. Nothing happened except for Penelopa singing Russian songs, and Piotr pacing and sighing heavily.

The interpreter got up. His knees ached. It was so stupid of him to come here. A huge waste of time. Anything was better than this, even the most boring interpreting, like for the physical therapists.

"Don't try to follow me," he said. "Or I'm calling the cops."

Piotr dropped his butt on the bed, deflated. If something did happen, he just aged a year or two.

"I think we should try again," Penelopa said. "If I add a few flakes of ground-up nutmeg..."

"You guys are nuts," the interpreter said, moving away without turning his back to her.

When he was at the door, he bent down and left an envelope on the floor.

When this guy who called himself the interpreter left, even before his footsteps faded into nothingness, Penelopa took another spoon of the serum and made a face. "Never thought it would taste so awful. Do you think the nutmeg would help?"

"Why did you let him go?" Piotr asked. "He has my pearls. Even if they don't work, they still have value. And he lied about being armed."

"Because I'm not into violence," she said. "I achieve results through my brain and not through my brawn. And it's not your pearls but ours."

She picked up the envelope the interpreter had left, and opened it up.

"Look, Piotr," she said. "And you said, violence..."

He lifted his eyes and saw on her palm three deep yellowish-orange pearls, reflecting his open-mouthed face.

"He left a note," she said. "I'm taking three pearls for myself. As a finder's fee."

"Three out of seven is too high," Piotr said. "The finder's fee is 20%."

"Piotr, I love you like a brother, like forty thousand brothers, but sometimes it's better if you just shut up."

An hour later, Penelopa drove the rented car back to New York while Piotr was riding shotgun.

"I think we should've kicked his butt until he returned us the other three pearls," Piotr said.

"Why don't you take a nap, Piotr?"

So, he did. He woke up flying, tumbling in the air. When he hit his head on the cloud and opened his eyes, the inside of his skull full of pain, he realized that the car had overturned and he was hanging upside down, held by his seat belt. He turned his head toward Penelopa. She was gone. Instead, there was a small girl, maybe ten, impaled on the steering wheel, embracing it with her tiny hands, staring at him. Her eyes were big on her bloody face. Blood was flowing on her deployed airbag.

"You're young, Piotr," she whispered.

And then the gasoline ignited.

At his daughter's house, the interpreter shared the news with his wife. "It didn't work."

"I told you so."

"You did, in a few words. But it was worth trying."

At my age, he thought, I know the value of words. Words can kill and words can heal. And they can even be the same words but in a different context.

He was about to voice out this platitude when she took his hand. They looked into each other's wrinkled faces, smiled, and kissed each other. And the twins rushed toward them and hugged them both.

As soon as they did, the interpreter's and his wife's wrinkles were gone, and all the pains and aches disappeared.

"Look," he said. "We are young again."

Mark Budman

"I told you. Kids make us young. No need for any stupid serum."

"Kids make us younger sounds like a Hallmark cliché."

"A cliché is true by definition."

"You can't know for sure. Maybe it was the serum."

"I didn't take any," she said.

"It was transferred to you through my kiss."

"You are a hopeless romantic."

"And you're the most beautiful grandma on Earth. I bet you they'd say you're the twins' mother."

"And that you are the twins' slightly older brother."

They got up, picked up a twin each, and walked together, hand-in-hand, young, healthy, and hopeful. Young not like the derisive caricatures in the interpreter's mind, but young in James M. Barrie's definition: "a little bird that has broken out of the egg."

And all the most excellent immigrants were happy for them, even the goldfish named Lyubov, who now swam merrily, merrily someplace far, far away.

Mark Budman is a first-generation immigrant. His writing has appeared or is forthcoming in *Catapult, Witness, Five Points, Guernica/PEN, American Scholar, Huffington Post, Mississippi Review, Virginia Quarterly*, and elsewhere. His novel **My Life at First Try** was published by Counterpoint Press. He co-edited multiple authors in anthologies from Ooligan and Persea presses, including the recent anthology of immigrant writing, **Short, Vigorous Roots.**